Luxury and Lies

Deborah Dickinson

Copyright © 2024 by Deborah Dickinson

All rights reserved.

No portion of this book may be reproduced in any form without written permission from the publisher or author, except as permitted by U.S. copyright law.

Contents

1. Chapter 1   1
2. Chapter 2   6
3. Chapter 3   11
4. Chapter 4   15
5. Chapter 5   21
6. Chapter 6   29
7. Chapter 7   34
8. Chapter 8   39
9. Chapter 9   43
10. Chapter 10   48
11. Chapter 11   54
12. Chapter 12   59
13. Chapter 13   66
14. Chapter 14   72
15. Chapter 15   78
16. Chapter 16   85
17. Chapter 17   92
18. Chapter 18   97

19.	Chapter 19	103
20.	Chapter 20	109
21.	Chapter 21	115
22.	Chapter 22	120
23.	Chapter 23	125
24.	Chapter 24	131
25.	Chapter 25	136
26.	Chapter 26	142
27.	Chapter 27	148
28.	Chapter 28	155
29.	Chapter 29	161
30.	Chapter 30	167
31.	Epilogue	173

CHAPTER 1

For over ten minutes, I stood in front of Hotel Invicta, a huge baroque building in the middle of the city. Six armed men guarded the place like it was some kind of palace.

I looked down at the invitation in my hands, a piece of pearly white paper so smooth that it felt like silk, with golden curly letters that read "Invicta applicant."

Hotel Invicta only existed for the wealthiest people in the world and was run by other rich people, who also were a little crazy and apparently bored as fuck in their lives because the things that happened in that hotel...

At least, if I were to believe all the absurd stories I heard the day before yesterday when my best friend suddenly called me up and told me about this place. Shana was her name, also known as Bentley, in the hotel. She worked here as a rewarder, and I was about to see her again for the first time after almost a year.

Invicta staff weren't allowed to contact people from their "old life," so we hadn't seen or spoken to each other since she took the job. The only reason she could contact me right now was that they were looking for a new rewarder, and Shana had convinced them that I could be a good asset to the hotel.

Honestly, they couldn't have contacted me at a better time!

So today, I would visit Invicta, and if things went well, I could stay there too, becoming a rewarder myself. I felt nauseous thinking about it, but I didn't have much choice.

It was either this or jail.

My phone started buzzing in my pocket. I picked it up.

"Are you coming in, or are you gonna stand there looking like you're gonna start puking any minute?!" Shana yelled in my ear.

"I'm still debating if I have my nerves under control. I might barf inside and ruin the million-dollar expensive carpet instead of the outside street, so I'm just trying to relax first."

"Get your shit together, woman. You want me to come down?"

"No. Yeah. Maybe."

"Choose one out of those three."

"Yeah... Please come down."

"Ugh, pussy. I'll be there in five."

Invicta wasn't just a "normal" hotel for the rich to stay in for a vacation. Oh no, it was something else.

There was a crazy world within that huge baroque building, where cops had no say—or maybe not even existed. Mike said that there was some sort of unwritten rule that made Invicta untouchable, and all its workers and guests got full immunity. Violence wasn't allowed in there, though, and would be handled by Invicta's own special "police." There was only one group that could use violence—a group of certain men.

Shana's job—and possibly my future one, too—was to please those certain men, working as a "slave" for them.

They were called gladiators. Strong men, competing against each other in the underground arena of Hotel Invicta to deliver a spectacle for rich people to gamble their money on.

Whenever a gladiator won, he got himself a rewarder as a prize, which he could keep for twenty-four hours and do whatever he wanted with them. There were only two rules. He couldn't leave marks unless there was another agreement, and he couldn't kill his prize. Further, he could do everything and ask for anything he wanted.

If gladiators wanted a rewarder to lick their feet, they must, or they wouldn't have done their job correctly and wouldn't get paid but punished instead.

And it paid well: a thousand dollars for twenty-four hours of work and a forever free stay at the hotel between working hours!

Not everyone could become a rewarder. Shana told me you need to have the brains and the looks.

I snapped out of my thoughts when the heavy-adorned golden door opened, and my friend waved at me, telling me to come in. It was so good to see her again!

"You're almost late; get your ass over here!" she shouted with a wide smile and her eyes a little glossed over. I knew she had missed me too.

"Well... here goes nothing..." I whispered before I dragged my feet towards the building door, where I showed the guards my invitation and was granted access.

After one huge hug, Shana brought me straight to the person I had an appointment with, and luckily, I was just in time. I couldn't see much of the hotel because we needed to make haste, but what I did see looked absolutely spectacular.

I was received by a woman who looked like she had walked straight out of a forties movie. Her name was Madame Gremelda. She was a beautiful woman, whom I guessed was around forty-five years old. Her warm auburn hair was wavy, pasted to her head, combed to one side, like how women used to do their hair a few decades ago.

Between her long fingers, she held a long black quellazaire, which was holding a cigarette at the end. She put the black tube between her shiny red lips and took an inhale.

Her office was so quiet that I could hear the cracking of the cigarette before she blew out some smoke. I had to prevent myself from coughing when the gray clouds hit my face.

She observed every inch of my face while she took a few other hoists and blew out a few other puffs.

I've never felt so stared at.

"Fery pretty indeed. Bentley vas telling zee truth..." she said, pleased, with the heaviest German accent I'd ever heard.

Shana—or Bentley like I had to call her in here—told me upfront that I needed to keep my mouth shut until I was asked a question, so I kept quiet.

When Madame Gremelda was done smoking and eyeing me, she stood up and slowly walked towards me, her hips swaying in her tight black dress with every step she took. She stopped just before me, grabbed my hair, and abruptly pulled my head back so I looked at her. It felt like she just snapped my neck in half, and I let out a loud cry from pain, but mostly because I hadn't seen this coming. The actual fuck?!

"Zat is ein fery schpecial moan you have zer," she whispered against my lips and suddenly stuck her tongue into my mouth. She tasted of mint and tobacco as she swirled her wet muscle in and around my mouth. I had no fucking idea what she wanted me to do, and I had never kissed another woman before. I didn't know what to do so I just went with her and kissed her back. She let go soon enough.

Thank God.

"Kood kisser too. Sehr gut..." she purred and returned to sit behind her desk again.

I swallowed and tried to catch my breath back. Honestly, this woman was a little scary. What the fuck was going on? What kind of job interview was this?!

Gremelda then looked at some papers I had to mail up front: an IQ test, my resume, school paperwork, and a medical certificate—all they had paid for.

She let out a long sigh and put the papers on a need stack again, which she then put in the top drawer of her desk.

"I am pleazed to inform you zat you are hired. Velcome to Hotel Invicta. Your new name schall be... Tesla," she said and stretched out her hand, which I shook.

Chapter 2

TESLA

After signing my new work contract, Shana showed me around at my new workplace.

Madame Gremelda had said I could go home to pick up my things, but it wasn't necessary since everything I needed would also be in the hotel room. I chose to stay as I didn't want to risk bumping into the cops at my place. The hotel was the safer option.

Invicta was huge and had the most luxurious interior I'd ever seen. The theme seemed to be black, white, and silver, and it all looked very expensive and elegant with those huge modern chandeliers hanging on high ceilings.

The guests I saw all looked like a million bucks, but Shana and I soon went a few levels higher to a unique floor where only staff stayed. I would mostly stay on this floor, never to mingle with guests as I hadn't come here for the guests. I came for the gladiators... It's still such a weird thing, gladiators in the twenty-first century.

"So this is your room. I begged you to have the room next to mine, and I succeeded! Who is the best?" Shana asked while she waited for me to open the door, using a key card.

Bleep. It opened.

"You are," I answered her with a nod. "Definitely you."

We entered my room, and my mouth popped open.

"Amazing, right?" Shana asked.

"Oh. My. Fucking. Lord." My voice echoed through the large room. This wasn't just a room; this was a fucking suite fit for a princess.

"Cool, huh, babe?"

"Is thid where I'll live for—for free?!"

"Yup."

"Alright, what's the catch, Shana? This just isn't possible!"

"Bentley."

"Huh?" I looked at her.

"You should call me Bentley from now on."

"Very well, Bentley."

"Anyway, what do you mean 'what's the catch?'" Shana asked. "You know what's the catch. You'll work as a slave for someone else."

"Yeah, but still... that's only for twenty-four hours, and it pays well too. But just look at this, woman!" I yelled, raising my arms. "I'd eat my own shit for this!"

"You say that now, but wait until you have to by request."

"It was just a matter of speech. Wait—I don't really have to eat my shit, right?! Why would a gladiator want me to do that?"

"What can I say?" Bentley shrugged. "There are some weirdos among them. I'm sorry, honey, but I've done some pretty crazy stuff since I started working here."

"Why'd you tell me that now instead of before?" I asked, suddenly feeling a little sick to my stomach. I seriously wasn't planning on eating my shit at all!

"It'll be fine. Besides, the most freaky of them isn't working. He's comatized in the hospital as we speak."

"Wow, really...? Is he in a coma because of a fight?"

"Yup."

"Wow, they're that rough? Like gladiators in the old times?"

"They can't murder each other as they did in the past eras. But yeah, they can get pretty wild. Last week, I saw a man bite off another guy's ear, and that's not even weird," Bentley explained while she gently closed the door behind us.

"What the fuck!?" I replied, walking further into the room.

"Yeah, and not like Mike Tyson, who only bit off a piece. I'm talking about the entire shell! And it was so fucking gross how he spat it out on the ground."

"Please, I don't wanna hear about these things anymore." I was thankful I at least wasn't obligated to watch the fights.

"Fine, I'll shut up," Bentley replied.

"Thank you."

I looked around a little while my friend poured us some drinks. When I finished, we took place on the luxurious leather couch. Everything in this room was incredible.

"I'm really happy to see you again," Bentley said.

"As am I."

"Are you gonna tell me what happened?"

"How do you know something happened?" I hadn't told her anything about what had happened.

"We might have missed each other for a while, but I'm still your best friend. I know when something's going on."

I put my drink on the table and rested my elbows on my knees, rubbing my face into my hands. "Later."

"Sure. I'm here, right beside you. We've never lived so close to each other." She caressed my back.

"I'm happy about that," I replied. "So, what's the deal with this hotel? Why is there no police allowed in here?"

No police around me was convenient for me, don't get me wrong, but it was still a tad weird.

"Let me explain something first," Bentley started. "Hotel Invicta is a chain of hotels located all around the world. Every guest here is part of the underworld—mostly mobsters, but also hitmen, bounty hunters, etcetera. They mostly stay here if they need to lay low. Invicta, however, is unbiased and gives guests what they require: protection, entertainment, privacy, or anything else. But in exchange, the guests have to bring in some big bucks. The cheapest room has five digits a night!"

Holy fuck?! I looked at her with an open mouth before I could speak again. "You have brought me to a place where murderers stay?"

"Yeah, but I can assure you that Invicta is probably the safest place in the world. Remember that no violence thing I told you about?"

I nodded.

"That's where Invicta's special 'police' come in," Bentley said, airquoting the word police. "If a guest misbehaves and doesn't follow the rules, he gets...well...taken care of."

"Like?"

"Mostly, they're getting finished. And not only the guest, their entire family."

How could my friend just speak about it like it was nothing? "What the hell?"

"So, you see, most criminals will be sure to behave well."

"Why is the police okay with this?"

"It's a win-win. If the guests don't behave, the police gets a dead criminal delivered at their door without doing anything while they're able to brag and take the credit."

I didn't know what to say. "Is this a fucking movie I ended up in or what?"

"Nah." She laughed. "Anyway, to give the guests something they can get a kick out of, the gladiators were introduced a few years ago. They're actually pretty important to the hotel, and that's also why you and I are here—hot, smart, sexy people—to entertain them and reward them for their hard work."

Chapter 3

TESLA

After some good hours of catching up with Bentley, I took a bath in my new luxurious bathroom, before getting ready. According to Invicta's contract and dress code, I should wear a black long dress.

There actually stood a lot in the contract. It was so much that I didn't read it all. I know that's stupid but I didn't really have much other choice then to be here. I fucked up and I really didn't wanna go to jail. Plus, I had my best friend here.

I wore black stockings, a black lingerie set underneath and picked a jewelry set out of the many pieces of jewelry I also got as a present. Jeez! This place really was something! I'd styled my hair in a way that I would have a bit of a curl.

My hands trembled from nervousness the whole time. Tonight will be my first night. The gladiators were fighting at this very moment and the winners of the day will get to choose a prize later. I and the other rewarders will be lined up like meat for sale and the best winner of the day can pick his prize first, then the runner up, and so on.

I wondered how it'll make me feel. Was I going to be relieved if nobody picked me or was I going to be offended they wouldn't be interested in me and thus had no means to make money?

I wasn't sure what I wanted more--to sleep alone tonight or not.

Bentley told me the number one Gladiator was a guy who's name is "Spartacus". Apparently, he was invincible. He always picked the same rewarder, though. A girl called Mercedes.

According to Bentley, Mercedes was "The Queen" of all Rewarders. Every Gladiator wanted her but they never got to have her because Spartacus always won and always picked her first.

Right when I hung some earrings in my earlobes, a knock on the door came.

"It's open," I answered.

My friend popped her head inside. "You ready to go?"

"Yeah." I tried to sound as normal as possible, but I was very nervous.

"Let's go then."

I checked myself in the mirror really quick and took a big inhale, filling my lungs with air before I exhaled again.

I could do this.

"You're fucking nervous aren't you?" Bentley asked while we stood in the elevator, going down.

It felt like it took ages. How far down were we going down? I felt hot already and it seemed like it only got hotter.

"I am. I'm so fucking nervous! What if some asshole picks me? And what if he demands all this crazy shit? I mean, you know I'm not averse to having a good cock in my mouth but...gosh...! What if the guy wants all these weird things?! What if he's gross?" I ran my hand through my hair in frustration and immediately regretted it.

My hair was looking so fine, I shouldn't mess it up! "What if he'll hurt me?! I mean, they can't inflict any kind of pain that leaves a mark, like biting or cutting skin, I've read that. But one can hurt someone without leaving any form of evidence on the body—"

"Jesus, breathe!" Bentley yelled as she grabbed me and shook my shoulders. "Gosh, it's mostly just fucking or even talking to the guy. Playing a game, having a fun day together. Even holding him while he cries about his ex he's still not over with. They aren't all nutjobs. I just wanted you to know that some can be, so you'll be prepared, but most guys are just normal guys. Fuck, now I regret what I said to you earlier..."

She looked at me with her large dark green eyes and I could tell she told me the truth.

"Really, they're mostly just normal?" I asked to be sure.

"Yeah... It's mostly just a nice cock in your mouth I know that you love so much. Ok?" she said with a gentle voice, patting my shoulders.

I took a big breath and tried to relax my body. "Ok, ok...yes."

The elevator stopped and Bentley was just done with fixing my hair while the doors slid open.

We had to walk through a hallway before entering a room.

Inside were more people, men dressed in all black with a white tie, and women dressed in long tight black dresses like Bently and myself.

It seemed like the Gladiators got a variety of flavors to choose from. From a chubby big breasted black beauty to a slim pale redhead to Asian petite twins (wait... do they come as a pair?) to a big muscled tattooed guy who looked like a Gladiator himself.

One thing was for sure, they were all so beautiful, they could be models. One girl was so gorgeous she stood out from the rest. That must be Mercedes. Her black hair was long and flowing like a waterfall over her back till it reached her hips. She had legs for days and a tiny waist with curves in all the right places.

"So when it's ten o'clock, which is in a few minutes, we'll line up and the winners will come to collect their Rewarder. Mostly about five winners will come."

I quickly counted and there were nine rewarders (or ten, I don't know if the Asians stayed together), so the chance I would get picked was at least fifty percent.

It made me nervous.

"Hey, you must be the new girl," a hot tanned guy asked me, I think he was Indian, if I had to guess. "I'm Mahindra," he said.

I shook his hand. "I'm...Tesla." It still felt so weird to say. "And yeah, it is my first day."

"Ok, cool. Well, good luck to—"

"Get ready, zey are coming," said a voice, cutting Mahindra off. I recognized it as Madame Germelda's before I could see her coming.

Her high heels clicked on the floor as she walked towards us and stopped before me to yank at my arm. "Schtand here," she ordered, putting me between Mahindra and buffed guy. I didn't know his name yet, so for now, he'll be buffed guy.

"Zis vill be your place in line from now on, ok? Remember zat for next time," Gremelda sternly said to which I nodded and replied to her that I understood.

A minute later, the doors swung open and half a dozen broad men entered the room, the dirt of the arena still on their muscled bodies.

Oh, fuck! It was time.

4

CHAPTER 4

SPARTACUS

After placing my bike against the fence, I reached into my pocket to get her gift out. My hands were sweating and my heart pounded inside my chest. Could I really do this?

I looked at the little black USB-stick that I held in my hand. For many hours this week, I'd been busy searching for the right music to put on it. I made a list of love songs and the first letter of each track spelled the following sentence: "Thanks for going out with me."

That's what I was here for, to ask her out on a date, and I begged God to let her say yes!

After inhaling and exhaling deeply, I forced myself to walk to the basketball court where I saw her standing, watching the game while smoking a cigarette. It was only her and two friends, who were in the middle of shooting some hoops.

Gosh, she looked so gorgeous. But she wasn't only beautiful, she was also smart, funny and kind. That's what made me fall for her before her looks. She'd always been nice to me.

When she saw me approaching her, she smiled. "Hey, Dean."

"Hey," I replied.

"Oh, you want a smoke too?" she asked, grabbing into one of her pockets.

In my eyes, smoking was her only bad habit. I normally didn't like smokers at all, but for her, I wouldn't mind the fact that kissing will be the same as licking out an ashtray. I'd gladly do it to feel her plump lips pressed against mine.

I shook my head.

"Oh, yes, you don't smoke," she said, putting the pack of cigarettes away. "I forgot... It's good you don't though."

We stood there for some time, watching the others while talking about unimportant stuff. I held onto the USB-stick like my life depended on it, telling myself that this was it, I should do it now, no way back.

"Would you wanna go out with me sometimes?" I asked and held my breath until she answered me.

"Oh, yeah, sure. I and the others actually are hanging out tonight and—"

"No...uhh...I actually meant... Would you wanna go on a--" I swallowed. "Date with me?"

"Oh," she answered and the way the short word came out of her mouth, felt like a slap in my face. This wasn't good, I knew it wasn't. "Well...I would like to hang out with you, but as friends...nothing more."

"Ok," I said, utterly disappointed. How foolish had I been? How could I possibly think that someone like her would want to go on a date with someone like me?

She sighed. "Dean—"

"No, not...uh, it's fine," I said and nodded, not wanting her pity. "I'm gonna go home then..."

"Oh, ok," she said, looking a tad uncomfortable.

I turned around and walked back to my bicycle as quickly as I could. The girl I was in love with for so long had just rejected me. The one I was in love with for the very first time in my life, just said no.

Fuck.

She didn't want me the way I wanted her and it felt horrible.

Only after I wanted to grab the handlebar of my bike, I noticed I still held tight onto the small flash drive in my hand. I looked at it and I didn't know why, but I wanted her to have it. It was made for her and I couldn't bear thinking about having to throw it away. I spent at least eight hours on that surprise.

I stepped onto my bike and drove to the basketball court.

With her back facing me, she talked about something, making her friends laugh real hard until the two noticed me and stayed quiet while she kept talking.

I wished she stopped talking when I heard what she was joking about.

"Like I want to go out with him. Come on Charlotte, Billy, you would have said no too." Her friends both shook their heads but she seemed to miss the hint. Oh, how I wish she would have taken the hint. "I mean, look at his crooked teeth and those pimples. And that long thin body. Like, his arms probably would make an orangutan jealous. And have you seen—" She suddenly stopped talking. "He...he"s right behind me, isn't he?"

Charlotte awkwardly nodded while Billy facepalmed and my crush slowly turned around, the shock noticeable in her eyes...

"Oh, hey, uhhh... Listen, Dean—"

"Don't," I ordered. I never felt so disappointed in someone before in my life.

She was supposed to be kind and sweet, just like her beautiful blue-green eyes were. But I didn't find her kind or sweet at all. She just crushed my heart.

"I'm so, so—"

"Here," I said, dumping the USB stick in front of her. It landed before her feet. "I've made it especially for you. I hope you like it."

I rode away, praying to wake up from this bad dream, but the truth was that this was real. Very real.

Eight years later

My God, why won't he just give up? As I sat on top of my opponent and my hands were busy beating the shit out of the guy, the audience went wild. They screamed and yelled for me to finish him.

"Just fucking give up, Gannicus," I whispered to him while hitting my fist against his cheek once more. I didn't wanna beat the living shit out of him but if he wouldn't quit, I didn't have any other choice.

Luckily, when I hit him again, he was finally knocked out. My knuckles hurt. Fucking Gannicus, why was he even trying? There was no way he could ever beat me anyway. Don't get me wrong, I respected his effort for trying but it was also just stupid and useless. After I got off him, I gave the audience a little show before the evening was over again. I was the winner, and Hotel Invicta gained plenty of bucks. Another day at the job fulfilled.

"Good match, man," Crixus said, putting his sweaty arm around me.

He was my best friend here and also the second-best fighter. He wasn't tall but he was very strong and the only one who almost beat me once. He was also the most eager to do so.

"Thanks. How did you do?" I asked.

"Second best," he said with a sour face, making me laugh.

"Let's go up, time to claim our prices."

He nodded. "Will you finally let me have Cedi?" he asked. Crixus always wanted to spend the night with Mercedes but he never got the chance yet.

"Nope," I answered.

"Gut match, boys, sehr gut. Time to claim your price," Madame Gremelda said after we entered the pinking room.

The Rewarders stood in line like they always stood, and Mercedes smiled at me, knowing she'll spend the night with the best again. She was my favorite, she was sweet, pretty, smart, and a good listener.

"Spartacus, you're in first place. You can choze first."

I stepped towards Mercedes and smiled at her. "I choose—" I don't know why, but my attention was pulled to the right, where my eyes met a pair of familiar ones. They were kind-looking and a beautiful shade of blue-green.

No, this couldn't be!

After all these years, it was her! What were the fucking odds that she stood here, offering herself to me as a Rewarder? The girl that didn't want me, now standing here to be at my mercy for twenty-four hours.

I stepped away from Mercedes, and it stung my heart a little when I saw her confused look. I was sorry for her, but I couldn't let this opportunity slip out of my hands. Above that, I wouldn't let any of the other Gladiators pick her.

In front of her, I stood still and observed her. Ryah looked at me with confused eyes, but I don't think she recognized me. How could she? I wasn't the thin, goofy, ugly guy with crooked teeth anymore.

"Ah, I zee you have interest in our newest Rewarder," Gremelda said. "Her name is Tesla."

"Tesla..." I replied. "I think it's time for me to take Tesla for a test drive," I said, winking at her. I saw she swallowed hard and I think her bottom lip just trembled even though she tried to hide it with an awkward smile. My heart pounded in my chest thinking about the next hours to come.

5

Chapter 5

Tesla

"So..." From behind me, a deep voice spoke and its owner shut the door with a bang. There we stood in his room, and my heart raced underneath my rib cage when I felt Spartacus's finger gently running over my spine. "...I gotta take a bath first," he said, walking past me.

I shivered at his touch and wondered what would happen after that bath.

As I followed him further into the room, I watched his gorgeous back muscles moving and flexing with every step he took. My eyes trailed from his shoulders to his waist and lower. He only wore a pair of brown leather pants to cover himself up, and honestly, it was hard to take my gaze off of him.

Five months... That's how long it had been since I got laid, and seeing a very attractive half-naked guy who also happened to just win a fight (and had earned a ticket to have his ways with me for twenty-four hours) made me feel not only nervous as fuck, but also hot as fuck.

It'll be alright, I told myself. Bentley had said that most Gladiators were just normal guys, so it's gonna be alright.

Spartacus turned around and cleared his throat. "I said I required a bath. I'll take a drink first."

It took me a few seconds before I came back to my senses, and I understood that he wanted me to run him his bath. When I looked up at his face after I stopped myself from staring at his perfectly sculpted pecs, I saw him looking at me with a raised brow.

"Oh! Y-yeah, sorry!" I said and rushed to the bathroom where I opened the water tap to fill the bathtub.

While the water was filling up the bath, I checked the temperature and grabbed a bottle of bath oil that stood on the edge of the tub. I smelled it and dumped a few drops of liquid in the water. It smelled like caramel but then a little spicy. It was nice.

When the bath was filled enough, I closed the tap. "Your bath is ready," I told Spartacus who had entered the bathroom in the meantime.

I wanted to leave to give him some privacy, but he grabbed my hand, making me stay. "Where do you think you're going?" he asked.

"Oh...Uh, I--"

He smirked and brushed some hair out of my face, tugging it behind my ear. His hands felt rough against my skin. Rough and strong, but also gentle.

As I looked into his eyes, they twinkled and they somehow seemed so familiar to me. I didn't know why. Have I seen him before? Have I seen those eyes before?

"You're not leaving my side, darling. You're my rewarder and will stay by my side until I tell you to leave," he told me. "So, Tesla...un dress me now."

Holy Jesus Christ.

Ok, I could do this. It's not like I never undressed or fucked a guy in my life. I'll show him my skills. While opening the button of his pants, my hands grazed against his abs, and shit, those muscles were hard as a brick. It didn't seem like Spartacus was going to help me any time soon with taking off those awfully tight leather pants, so I sunk to my knees and pulled them down his legs, trying not to gaze at the visible bulge that was shown inside his white boxer briefs.

Damn.

Finally done with those damn pants, I pulled his underwear down and I swear that I didn't mean to stare at it for so long...but, I did...

"Like what you see?" he asked and I coughed in response, almost choking on my own spit.

"..."

"Can't blame you." He smirked. "I'm pretty happy with it myself." He stepped into the bathtub and slowly sat down, sinking in the water. A satisfied moan escaped his lips. "Ahh...this feels nice."

The next few minutes I stood beside the tub, not knowing what I should do. What was expected of me? Talk to him? Offer him something? Wait till he asks me to do some--

"Undress yourself, then turn around, spread your legs and bend over for me."

"...!"

"Take off your dress and underwear. Turn around, then spread your legs for me and bend over." He said again when I hadn't moved.

Ok, that was direct...

"O-oh...ok," I said, stuttering like an imbecile. Oh, come on, Ryah, you knew this was going to happen!

With my heart hammering inside my chest, I first unzipped my dress and let it fall to the ground. I tried to at least be a little sexy about it but I think I looked like a moron instead. I almost fell to the floor when I plucked the stockings from my legs. I then took off my bra and panties and turned around."Spread and bend over." It's not like I'm a prude. I've shown myself to many men. I'd stripped for boyfriends and one-night-stands, danced for them, gave little sexy shows for them, but for some reason, I felt shy in front of this guy. Maybe a little insecure. I mean, I was nowhere near as hot as that Mercedes girl and I also don't think I've ever hooked up with a hot guy like him before. Mostly I just hooked up with attractive guys but this man was just super hot...

I slowly spread my legs and decided I shouldn't overthink things and will just show him what I got. So, I bent over, showing him all of me.

"That's a nice pussy," he praised. His voice seemed more hoarse than before. "You're beautiful."

"Well, thank--"

"Play with yourself a little," he ordered. When I briefly looked through my legs, I saw him watch me as he took a sponge and started soaping up his godlike body.

I debated if I found this situation hot or not, but figured that in the end, it didn't really matter because I was here to serve him and gained a thousand bucks by that, so touching myself didn't seem to be that bad.

I pushed a finger inside, slicked it up, and searched for my clit, before I started to masturbate in front of his eyes. It had been long since I had done this for someone and I don't think I ever did it in such a vulnerable position before.

After a while, Spartacus pulled the plug out of the tub and stood up. I looked at him through my legs again and saw his cock was hard as he walked to the shower to wash the soap off his body. It felt so forbidden what I was doing and the fact he was hard by watching me made me feel horny beyond words. I was starting to get some good tingles in my nether regions as my clit started to swell underneath my massaging circling fingers.

"Ahh..."

"You truly haven't noticed it do you?" he asked when turned off the shower.

I was confused. "See w-what?" I asked, while still vigorously rubbing over my clit. Fuck, it felt so good, I couldn't deny that.

"Me." He walked towards me till he stood in front of me and slapped my hand away from my pussy, only to replace it with his own.

"Hahhh...!" I gasped at the sudden touch. "Y-you?" I managed to ask while his fingers started to caress me.

I almost came right then and there.

"Hmm-hmm, me," he whispered against my ear while one hand was placed on my shoulder and his other pushed inside of me. "You and I...we've met before."

"W-we have? Ahh..."

"Stand up straight." I did as he ordered but almost fell down because my legs trembled so much. "Eight years ago, at the basketball court..." He said as he hoisted me up and walked us over to the bed where he threw me on the mattress.

I could observe his cock from up close and it was so hot. It stood up high and thick, all veiny and engorged, just the way I like a dick to be--aggressive and angry. "A boy," he continued, snapping me out of my stare. "Known to be ugly, with pimples and crooked teeth, and freakishly long arms..."

Flashes of old memories crossed my mind. Oh, God. It couldn't be him, could it?

"That boy grew out to be a man," Spartacus growled while he pushed my legs apart. "But he never quite forgot the words he heard on that one fateful day."

"D-dean?" I asked, stuttering. Could this man really be high school Dean?

"It's Spartacus now, Tesla... Just like I can't call you Ryah in here, you can't call me Dean," he answered while looking at my stretched open pussy with lust in his eyes.

His eyes...that's why they were familiar! It was him. It really was him. What were the odds of us meeting again?! This place wasn't even in the same city as our old school. It was a four-hour drive.

"What...what are you gonna do to me?" I asked, recalling how I had been the biggest bitch ever that day.

"Don't worry, I won't hurt you..."

He pushed me flat against the bed and hovered over me.

"I...n-never got to tell you how sorry I was that day in March," I spoke truthfully.

I was young and stupid that day we'd last saw each other, but that didn't make my actions less wrong. I remembered the look on his face the moment I had turned around he stood there, behind me. I still felt so awful thinking about it.

That evening, I felt so nauseous. I couldn't stand myself and I eventually fell asleep after telling myself that I should apologize to him the very next day, but he never came back to school. It was awful to realize how my horrible attitude had driven a gentle and nice boy away from school.

"You do remember?" Spartacus asked and his voice was a little softer.

"I do--ahh!" he just slipped two or three fingers inside of me.

This has got to be the weirdest foreplay I've ever had in my life. I clutched at his shoulders and squeezed them, caressing over his muscles. It felt awkward that it felt this good.

"Of course, I remember you... I l-listened to your music that same evening and believe me if I tell you that I felt horrible. I s-still feel horrible. I wanted to apologize to you...but you were gone, and I never saw you at school again..." I breathlessly explained while he was fingering me at high speed, grazing over my G-spot again and again while dirty wet sounds bounced off the walls.

I threw my head to the back at the incredible feeling he gave me. "Ahh, f-fuck..."

Spartacus slid down between my legs and while his fingers kept thrusting in and out of me, his other hand pulled up my folds, till my clit came out to his full attention which he began to lick and suck, assaulting me at two different places, simultaneously. His tongue was soft yet demanding and the way he sucked on it was something I'd never felt before. It was so intense."Oh, G-god! Shit," I hissed, running my hands through his wet hair. It didn't take long for me to reach the point of coming.

Jesus, he was skilled. I've honestly never been eaten out like this. I felt my stomach tighten, ready to climax until he stopped fingering me and took his mouth away from my throbbing clit. My body shivered all over. Right at the moment before coming, Spartacus stopped his movements. "J-jesus, ahh."

"I'm still gonna make you pay for that day..." he said softly, coming up and closer, breathing against my lips with his wet slippery ones.

He gently kissed me and I don't think I ever felt hornier than at this very moment. I was pretty sure I whined when he just let go of me. "I've got all night to play with you... But, if you give me the name of one song that was on my playlist, I'll let you come more than once before the twenty-four hours are over, and you can count on me if I say I'm gonna be the best you've ever had."

I swallowed hard.

"You got five seconds," he said. "One..."

Fuck, I couldn't think straight when he grazed his pelvis against my clitoris again!

"Two..."

"Oh, God. Uh...."

"Three..."

"That one s-song!"

Fuck what was it called?!

"Four..."

At the very last second, I blurted out the name of a song and I was positive that my answer was correct.

And I knew it was, when I saw him smiling, even if it was only for a millisecond.

6

CHAPTER 6

SPARTACUS

Crixus came walking towards me and slapped me on my back, "I don't know what possessed you to not pick Mercedes at the last picking round, but hey, thanks!"

I laughed. "So, you two had fun?"

"Oh, yeah."

"Do you think she was very pissed at me?" I asked.

"I dunno, but I don't think so, cause she was too busy moaning out my name."

I suspected that she was probably upset with me, however, I didn't owe her anything and she could praise herself lucky for having the opportunity to be my Rewarder for so long, but now I had found another favorite and I'd pick Tesla before I'd pick Cedi any day. She was a nice girl and all, but Tesla...Ryah...she was my weakness. She was still my weakness... I found that out two nights ago.

I smirked, thinking back about the hours we'd spent. How I'd pleasured her, or perhaps some would call it punishment...

"Oh, God. I can't take it anymore," she cried out.

"What can't you take anymore, darling?"

We were at it for four hours and both still hadn't come, even though she must have been close to peaking at least ten times. I fingered, licked, and fucked her. I did it all. She tasted so good. This was torture to me as well.

"I...S-spartacus, please," she begged. "Dean--"

"What did I tell you?" I asked while kneeling beside her and shoving my cock inside her again. "Don't call me Dean in here."

"I'm s-sorry. Oh, God... I can't hold back," she whined and I slowed my pace and took my fingers away from her clit. "I... I told you the name of the song. I said I was sorry... Ahh, I need to come--"

"True. And I said that you will, but I didn't say when now did I?"

The truth was, I could keep her on the edge for as long as I allowed it, something taught to me by Harriet, the first lover I ever had. She was an older lady at forty-two while I had just turned eighteen. She was gorgeous and taught me everything I needed to know when it came to activities in the bedroom, and delaying orgasms was no exception as she was a fan of that herself.

I did put my Rewarder out of her misery after about five hours, I'm not a bad man after all.

And, oh, how it was so beautiful when she came. She even cried out my name in the moment of passion. I was pretty sure it was the most intense orgasm she'd ever experienced and it will make her think about me, wishing for me to pick her next time, I was sure of that. And that idea felt pretty awesome.

"Well... You look pretty satisfied yourself as well," Crixus said, smiling so wide I could see all his teeth. "Does this mean you're gonna let me have her more often?"

"Oh, you can have her anytime, buddy."

"Wow. That new girl was that good?"

Honestly? No, she wasn't that good at all, I mean, it was me who did all the work after all. "Let's just say that she cast a spell on me," I answered.

Crixus opened his mouth, but before he could speak, it was our doctore who entered the arena.

A doctore was the title of a trainer of Gladiators in historical times. Because we kinda do the same thing here, we call our trainer our doctore as well. Oenomaus was his name.

When Oenomaus stepped on the sand of the arena, fun was over and it was time for practicing. We trained every day for hours. Our fights were very real but Oenomaus taught us how to best handle the fights, where to hit to hurt someone without doing too much damage, stuff like that.

We mostly practiced a different kind of skill every day. It wasn't always fighting with our bare hands, as we did in the last match. Sometimes we fought with weapons, like swords, spears, knives, and sticks. And on other days we practiced for special fights. An example of such a special fight is that a stronger gladiator would be blindfolded and had to fight a weaker opponent, who was without a blindfold. I always hated those kinds of matches and training to the core, since it was I who ended up wearing the blindfold, and it just sucked.

Luckily it wasn't one of those horrendous days, because Oenomaus had other attributes with him.

"We will practice with the net and trident today!" he yelled.

That made me smile because the net and trident were one of my favorites.

"Ugh..." I heard a huge sigh coming from the person standing next to me. Seemed like they weren't Crixus's favorites at all.

"I still can't believe I was buried ten inches deep inside that one," Crixus said while eye-fucking Mercedes, who sat at the other side of the bar.

"Jesus. Why do you always have to be so vulgar, man? And ten inches? Who are you even trying to impress here?"

I saw Cedi looking at me a few times, but I didn't know what to say to her, so I didn't get up to talk to her. Luckily, she and I never really had much contact outside of the hours she worked for me, hence, it wasn't strange we didn't talk now, but still...something didn't sit completely right with me. I didn't want her to feel like she was dumped by me or anything, even though she kinda was...

Crixus snapped me out of my thoughts when he suddenly laughed out loud again, letting his head fall back. He seemed to do that a lot today--smiling and laughing.

"I'm just...still not over that night."

Suddenly, I realized something. He'd never told me before, but... "Crixus, do you like the girl?" I asked.

"What? Pffff... You know we aren't allowed to date anyone from the hotel."

"That wasn't my question."

"I just think she's a great girl."

"You can talk to her too, you know. You don't have to sit here with me."

"I like to sit with you," he answered. "Look, I had a great time with her. Ok? But right now I'm with my buddy."

A great night, he said... I had a great night too, and speaking of that great night, the one I'd spent it with, just came walking through the door. She and that other Rewarder--I think Bentley was her name. They took place at one of the tables and ordered drinks.

While Crixus and I talked about tomorrow's fight, my eyes kept searching for Tesla's and when hers and mine met, I raised my glass in the air. She let out an awkward smile and then tried to do the same, but she knocked over her glass and spilled the drink all over the table.

I smirked. In my memory, Ryah was nowhere near clumsy, but maybe I just think about her that way because to me she was a God-like creature in highschool. It wasn't just her beautiful appearance. She'd always been a genuinely nice girl. At least, until that one day...

I was most disappointed in her behavior back then, not even in the way she saw me. Just the disappointment of her--a girl who'd always been so nice and sweet--suddenly being such a mean person, insulting me to the core.

However, after the hours we spent together this week, I couldn't be angry with her anymore and I forgave her. I wouldn't ever forget her words, but I realized we were just young back then. What she had done was still wrong, but hadn't we all done a regrettable thing in our lives? I'd made mistakes too. At least she apologized to me.

She looked at me with red cheeks while wiping up the wet mess using her napkin. I smiled at her. No, Ryah had never been a klutz, but maybe I was the reason that Tesla was one now?

Chapter 7

TESLA

"Your first time vas ein zucces. Spartacus has told me he vas very pleased with zee new Rewarder."

"He said that?" I asked and I couldn't help but feel happy after hearing that Spartacus seemed to be pleased with the hours we'd spent together.

"Hmm...fery pleased. Therefore, we have depozited zee money to your Invicta account."

"That's great, thanks."

"Off you go, Tesla," Madame Gremelda said and she waved at the door of her office.

I guess that was my cue to leave. "Thank you."

On the way back to my room, I thought about the money I'd make every time I got to work. The hotel had opened a special "Invicta account" for me since all my ties with the "normal" world were broken.

The hardest part of that was not being able to see my parents. I'd told them I was traveling around the world and they seemed to believe me so for now I was safe.

I would get a thousand dollars on my account, each time I was picked as a Rewarder and it'll be saved there until I quit the job. I can spend it too, of course, but there isn't much I can buy in the hotel and we weren't that often allowed to go outside. Only a few days a year was what Bentley had told me. I hadn't asked Gremelda about it, though. There were a lot of things I hadn't asked her... Maybe I should read that contract a little better. Or not, cause I thought to myself that it might be better to know as little as possible about hotel Invicta. Honestly, it seemed to be one major fishy business if I was to say something about it.

Fishy or not, for now, I was happy. It had been the fastest thousand bucks I've ever made in my life. If it was the easiest? I don't know. It was hard as he tortured me for hours, but it was a sweet kinda torture. It was a torture that even kept me up in the nights that followed, not able to get the thoughts out of my head.

God, damn! It even took hours until I stopped feeling him inside of me.

How could that man be Dean from school? Thinking about Dean made me remember what a bitch I had been to him. I really did hate myself for my actions that day, wishing I could turn back the clock. It was a relief to finally be able to say I'm sorry to him. I had been wanting to tell him those words so badly.

With my head still full of thoughts, I opened the door to my room and almost got a heart attack when Shana sat there on my couch watching tv!

"Jesus, fuck, Sha--I mean Bentley! What the fuck are you doing in my room?!"

"Oh, I used the spare key," she answered, not looking up. There was a program going on about penguins and I knew her love for them birds.

"Spare key?"

"Yeah, you received two key cards."

"Then why did you give me only one?" I asked, crashing next to her.

"Well, duh...cause I kept the other one."

"Why would--you know, nevermind. Keep it."

When the baby penguin hatched from the egg, Bentley paused the program and turned to me, looking at me with grey twinkling eyes when she asked, "What did she say? Was she pleased?"

"Yeah, she said Spartacus was very happy with my services."

I was so proud to say these words.

Bentley slapped against one of my shoulders. "I knew you would be perfect! This is great, now she'll be happy with me too, cause I was the one who recommended you! Let's grab a drink at the bar to celebrate."

Turned out that we celebrated more nights at the bar than only that night, and tonight there was a familiar face sitting on one of the barstools. He raised his glass to me, and when I wanted to do the same, I made a stupid mistake.

"Shit."

I saw his smirk after the content from my glass dripped down, soiling my pants. Why, oh why, did I have to knock over the glass precisely when he was looking at me?

While I was dabbing myself and the table dry, my friend explained another rule to me.

"I can see that blush on your cheeks and I don't know the deal about you and him, but keep in mind you can't date," Bentley said while she stood up and used her napkin too.

"Hm?" I looked at her as innocently as possible. Me blushing, pff, no way. "Date? Why would you say that?" I asked.

"Cause I know you, and I can see you find him more than interesting. But, as I said, no dating. Or Gremelda will slit your throat or something. Frankly, I don't even know if that's a lie or not, she'll probably do it."

"Well, I wasn't planning on dating anyway, I'm just here for the job."

"Hm, the job and the thing you still haven't told me about," she said while taking her seat again.

"I will...later."

"I know. The bar isn't the place for heavy stuff anyway. I just wanted to let you know that I haven't forgotten about it."

One of the waitresses came to clean up the mess I made. I apologized to her and ordered new drinks.

"But uh...why the no-dating-policy?" I asked while secretly checking out the guy sitting a few meters further.

Flashes of him and I being busy in his bedroom came to my mind again and they gave me a certain strange feeling inside my stomach. I coughed and looked at Bentley again, who looked at me with a raised brow.

"What's wrong?" I asked.

"Your mouth hung open the entire time you were ogling him."

"W-wha--I wasn't ogling him!"

"You so were. And if I see it, he definitely sees it. Maybe that's why he is wearing that arrogant smile the whole time." I wasn't ogling. Bentley exaggerated. "Anyway...Gladiators and Rewarders aren't allowed to date each other, I have no idea why not. I think it has something to do with a Gladiator only having his focus on the matches or whatever."

"Ok," I replied. Strange rule.

When it was around one o'clock, Bentley and I said goodnight to each other and she went to her room while I went to mine.

After taking a shower, I went to bed.

In all honesty, the night I slept next to him was the only night that I had slept more than four hours since...since weeks. Ever since it happened, I haven't been able to sleep. But with Spartacus, I slept. Man, I slept like a baby. The fact I was completely drained from every juice and energy I had in my body possibly had something to do with it too.

I think I really should tell Bentley the reason why I wanted to come to a place like this in the first place. I wanted to tell her. I will tell her. Tomorrow.

Chapter 8

SPARTACUS

I couldn't help but wonder what it was that had brought Ryah to the Hotel because I think that no person who's in their right mind would work for a company like Invicta. I knew why I was here--for the money. But why was she here?

It was almost time for the fight tonight and I did what I always did before a fight, or at some other point in the evening: I logged in to watch my brother. He's the reason why I'm working here. Normally, contact with the outside world is forbidden for workers of the hotel, but this wasn't really contact anyway, so Gremelda allowed it. Also because I'm her star Gladiator at the moment. That's not me being arrogant, it's just the truth. And besides that, my brother couldn't see me, I could only see him. It's not like we talked or communicated in any other way.

"Goodnight, big brother," I said after one of his nurses had laid him in bed. He'll sleep soon.

I logged out right before a loud knocking came on my door. "Showtime!" Crixus yelled from the hallway. I opened the door and he looked rather unhappy. "I so don't wanna fight with that fucking trident and net, man."

"Oh, It'll be fun. Maybe I'll let you kick my ass in the first round...will that make you smile again?"

In the first round, I could lose. In fact, in that round, I sometimes had to lose to bring in some cash as a lot of people bet on me winning. I, however, refused to lose the final round.

"It's no fun if you let me win," Crixus whined while we walked towards the elevator. I smirked as we stepped in and pressed the button to go down.

In the wagering room, bets were called every time they were placed by the guests, coming in every few seconds. Loud rings went off and echoed through the room as the staff was busy typing in every newly placed bet. It was always a very busy happening. I saw numbers appearing on the screen with as many as six zeros. I mean, I'm talking about millions! Really, people were always fucking crazy when it came to gambling their money but the richest in the world were even crazier.

Spartacus/Crixus 12-1, Spartacus/Gannicus 9-0, Spartacus/Crixus 8-3, Spartacus/Flamma 8-7

Shit, it felt good to be the favorite of the audience.

"What?! 12-1, what the hell? People have no fucking faith in me, I tell you!" Crixus cried out, irritated as fuck.

Sometimes I wondered how much money would be made during one evening but I'd never dared to investigate that. I knew Gremelda would never tell me anyway, but I bet it was a shitload of cash.

Us, fighters, liked to come here before the matches to get a little kick out of it. Gremelda never let us stay long, though.

"Off you go akain, gentleman. Oenomaus is already vaiting," she said while observing the screen with all the bets very thoroughly.

She was responsible for the Gladiators, their fights, the gambling cash that came flowing in, and the Rewarders. So, it was mostly with her if we had to deal with someone at the hotel. I'd never seen the big boss while I was already here for almost two years. I think I didn't even wanna see the big boss, though. I bet he's no joke...

The other boys and I walked to the back where Oenomaus was waiting for us already. He gave some pep talk like he always did and the first round began.

While watching the other men fight, waiting till it was my turn, my eyes caught someone sitting in the audience. I couldn't believe that she came to watch. During our spent hours together she told me she didn't like violence and it seemed to me that I shouldn't count on seeing her in the arena, yet, here she was. Her eyes scanned the arena and when she had finally found mine, I winked at her.

She smiled at me and I just knew she was here for me.

I hated that I had to lose one of the first rounds, especially now Tesla was watching. I couldn't stand that she might not know I was faking it. I'd never lose a battle against Flamma.

When the final match came, it was me against Crixus. Poor guy. I whispered in his ear I'll finish him soon and he told me to fuck off.

I loved Crixus like a brother and a part of me pitied that he had to lose again, especially because Cedi sat in the audience, and even though he said he didn't like her, I knew he did. It made me wonder how I was so blind to never have seen it before. Or did he fall head over heels for her after their first night together?

In the end, it didn't matter because it was forbidden anyway.

"Begin!" Oenomaus shouted and he let his whip clash against the sand. Wuh-PSSSH!

This was purely for the show though, we've never been whipped even once, but I had to admit he looked kinda cool like this.

Like I already thought, Crixus was an easy opponent. For the sake of the show, I let him punch me a few times and have him throw the net upon me before I returned the favor and caught him in my net until he had no way to escape anymore. I then stabbed the trident between the ropes, faking it, of course, I wouldn't impale him for real. When we fought with our fists or wooden sticks or blunt weapons like that, we fought for real but during evenings with actual metal weapons, we always had little bags of blood within our clothes and those were the ones I aimed for.

Blood gushed through the air and fell upon the sands while Crixus let out cries and screams in anguish. I pulled the net off of him and punched him a few times on the nose because, hey, this is still a fight.

"Fucking, asshole," he cursed, breathlessly. "What the hell? Fucking arrogant prick--"

I knocked him against his face once more. Ok, I might have shown off a little bit there. I just wanted Tesla to see me at my best, at my strongest. I looked at her but I couldn't really read her facial expression. Was she impressed or repelled? I guess we have to find that out tonight when she'll be my Rewarder again.

Because in the end, I won the match 12-1.

9

Chapter 9

SPARTACUS

After a bath, I sat down beside Tesla on the bed. Nothing had happened yet, I purposely didn't make a move on her. I also wasn't planning on making a move, actually. Maybe I'll let her crave for me tonight. She was watching some tv like I had instructed her to do until I was done washing the arena sand from my body. Since we had better things to do now, I grabbed the remote control and switched off the program. There was immediate silence in the room.

"Let's play a little game," I suggested.

"A game?" Tesla bit at her upper lip and it looked so fucking hot. That had always been a thing for me when it came to sexiness--women who bite their lips. I have no idea why, but where other people had a thing for nipples, veins, feet, or whatever, I had a thing for lips that were stuck between teeth getting all plump and red and wet.

"Yeah, let's pretend we're young again and play truth or dare," I answered, almost getting a hard-on.

"Oh, I always hated that game," she said.

"Well, I'm your master for the next twenty-two hours and I'm telling you that we're gonna play it," I said, rather sternly, and sat up straighter to take a sip of apple juice. Tesla softly chuckled. "What?" I asked.

"Nothing...only that it's still a bit strange to see a man like yourself drinking from a juice box."

"Hey, I love apple juice, ok?"

Her green-blue eyes shimmered as she nodded and took a sip of wine herself.

"I'll give you the advantage to start," I said.

Wasn't I a good sport?

"Ok," she replied. "Truth or dare?"

"Let's just start with truth," I answered.

She licked his lips and thought about her question for a few seconds. Enough time for me to observe her. She'd changed a bit in those eight years we hadn't seen each other, but not so much. I could still easily recognize her from her seventeen years old self. Of course, her face had become more mature, but there wasn't much change and even the little features that had changed, had made her only more beautiful.

She had longer hair now than he had in high school. But both longer and shorter hair suited her in my eyes. She was so beautiful.

"This is actually pretty hard," she said, sighing. "Ok, I have a question. How long are you here? I mean in hotel Invicta?"

"Almost two years. Ok, my turn."

"Ok, I want truth too." She grabbed her glass of wine and took a few sips while she waited for me to ask her the first question.

"In the past few days, have you masturbated thinking about our night together?" I asked, making Tesla choke on the wine. The poor girl started coughing uncontrollably. Maybe I should pity her, but I kinda didn't. I gently patted her back and when she was done coughing, I said, "and this is a game of truth. Remember that you can't lie."

She closed her eyes and scrunched her nose in shame when she admitted it. "I...did..."

It looked so cute. When she opened her eyes again, she found me smirking at her and her cheeks blushed for me.

"You again, I'm doing another truth." She whispered something so soft, and I really couldn't make anything out of it. "What?" I asked.

"I asked if...you...had done that yourself?" she asked, not looking at me.

"Have I jerked off with you in my mind? Is that what you mean to ask me?" I asked rather loudly.

"Hmm-hmm," she hummed, looking everywhere except at me.

"I have," I answered. That was the truth. I so had. "Couple of times actually."

"...!"

She quickly grabbed her wine again and gulped the drink down till the glass was empty.

After a few more innocent and flirtatious truths and dares, I was suddenly in a more serious mood when Tesla picked truth again.

"Why did you say those things about me?"

She immediately knew what I was talking about. "I really don't know...Like I said before, I was young and a stupid fuck. I guess I just wanted to be funny with my friends. Even though it wasn't funny at all. It was just so stupid and wrong."

She got that right. "Tell me how awful you felt afterward," I said, wanting to tease her. Maybe I was a little mean.

Tesla turned her head and looked at me. "I felt so awful. I felt like shit. I still feel like shit when I think about it. Have you ever felt shame and regrets about something? It feels horrible. You know you're to blame and you wish you could turn back time, but you can't. You hate yourself for what you've done. And hating yourself is just horrible..."

"I don't think I ever felt ashamed like that," I answered. Luckily, I haven't.

"Because you're kind. Even though you're working as a fighter, I still think you're a nice man. You must have hated me so much...I mean...I guess you hated me enough to move and never return to school again."

She looked down at her hands in shame, picking at her cuticles. Her nails and the area around them were a mess. She must pluck at her skin all the time, and her nails looked like she bit them too.

"I wasn't too happy with you, but you weren't the reason I never came back to school," I answered while I stopped her hand from plucking at the skin. "Don't do that. Your fingers already look like a mess. It looks painful, the way you're messing up your skin there. It's not lady-like." "Whatever...as if a man can bite his nails and a woman can't." She rolled her eyes.

"It's a bad habit for both," I said and she looked at me again. "You really didn't leave school because of me?"

"I left because my family moved. We went to another town for my dad's work and because there were better facilities for my brother there," I explained.

"Oh, yes, your brother had an accident, didn't he?"

"Yeah, he got into a car accident."

"I remember you often spoke about him. Milo, right?" she asked and I nodded. I couldn't believe she remembered my brother's name too. She had a good memory for someone that I thought had never noticed me. "How is he now? You can't see him while being here, can you?"

"I can't talk to him, but I have access to see his room if I want to. We agreed at a certain time in the evening for me to check up on him."

"That's good, I guess."

I had told myself this evening that I wasn't gonna give her any, but I suddenly had such a desire to kiss her, that I laid my hand on her face and turned her so she looked at me. Her breathing accelerated and mine did too. Call me crazy, but I think we were having a moment here.

She swallowed again and I leaned in to kiss her neck. I felt it bob underneath my lips as she swallowed again and licked up to her jaw before I traced my lips higher.

"Tell me the truth. If you weren't supposed to please me as a Rewarder, would you wanna kiss me right now?" I whispered in her ear while I let one of my hands run through her hair.

"You're so d-direct with your questions," she said before she let out an awkward laugh.

"You think so?" I asked, sucking on her earlobe.

"Hmm-hmm."

"You haven't answered my question, though..." I said, kissing her neck again. I could feel little goosebumps appearing underneath my tongue.

"F-fuck," she cursed. "Yeah, I would."

I smiled. "I already knew you would," I replied before I finally let my lips melt with hers.

10

Chapter 10

TESLA

I was the first to wake up, and it wasn't in my own bed that I lay. It was in Spartacus's, where I'd spent the night. I laid against him and could smell the scent of his hair. It smelled like that oil he had in the bathroom--caramel with something else.

It smelled so good.

I wondered how late it was since it was already light, so I rolled away from him to check my phone. It was ten am! Oh my God, I couldn't believe I'd slept the whole night without waking up once!

Last evening, we kissed for the better part of one whole hour where I kept waiting for him to order me to undress, but...he didn't.

And that kinda...sucked? I think it did. I'd rather have sucked on something else, no shame in that. If that makes me a deprived slut, then so be it. I couldn't help myself, I was deprived. I didn't have sex for months until he showed me how he could work my body a couple of nights ago.

Of course, I would never just tell him that, but I wished I would have had the guts last night to tell him.

I sighed while I turned to my side, propped up on my elbow, and looked at him. He slowly breathed, facing the other side of the room, turned away from me. His body was covered underneath the duvet but one could easily see his posture. He was so massive, I couldn't believe that this man used to be the skinny guy from high school. I mean, just look at him now, he was huge.

Large in more than one place...

His shoulders were so broad, I wouldn't be surprised if I could fit in them twice. His skin had a beautiful natural tan and his hair was shiny black and fell to the sides of his face. He usually wore it to the back with some gel but right now it looked so soft.

He had a beard too. Not a full long one, but a trimmed one. A hot beard. I never really like beards but I think he looked good with his one. I think I might suddenly have gotten a secret beard kink or something. That night--when we did get past kissing--I felt his beard tickle against my skin, also when he was working his tongue down there. I liked it, the little prickles it gave me. It turned me on just thinking about it. Just thinking about his lips against my--

"Are you done ogling me?"

My eyes grew wide. "Y-you're awake?"

"Hmm-hmm."

"I wasn't ogling you."

What is it with people accusing me of ogling him these days? First Bentley wouldn't shut up about it and now Spartacus himself had asked me. I was just looking at him. I looked at a lot of people.

"It's ok, you can ogle me if you want," he mumbled, his face still looking in the other direction with his eyes closed.

"I don't need to ogle you."

He turned around to look at me. Jesus Christ, it should be forbidden for someone to look this good when waking up!

"Oh...but I like it when you do," he replied.

I let myself fall on my back and watched the ceiling. "Well, I wasn't."

"You should. Cause..." he rolled over till his face was so close to mine that I felt his warm breath against my ear. "...You should memorize every inch of me. You can use it for your naughty daydreams later."

"..."

I felt my face getting redder with each second, thinking back about how I admitted to fantasizing about him.

He smiled and got out of bed. "You're cute like that. I'm gonna get up, brush my teeth, and maybe if you're lucky...I'll give you more than just a kiss..." he said, winked, and walked out of the room.

I scoffed. "You're the boss, do what you want..." I mumbled and I heard him laugh.

When he was in the shower, I got out of bed and paced around in the room, I just couldn't sit or lay still. If I wouldn't have known better, I would say I was nervous, but that would be totally ridiculous.

Nothing's going on, Ryah, you might get lucky and get fucked so, so thoroughly. It's all good.

The thought of his cock inside of me made me beyond horny. Or to have it in my mouth! It made my stomach flutter... I hadn't even sucked him off the last time and that was my special skill. Men loved it when I sucked them off. They always said I was best at it.

"It's all yours..." I heard a voice behind me.

I turned around, presuming he was talking about his cock while he stood deliciously naked in front of me so I could kneel before him, but...

He was all dressed.

Oh.

"Tesla..." He smiled. "I meant the bathroom, it's yours to get in. Are you disappointed I'm dressed?"

"Hm?" I looked at him, shaking my head a bit and pretending to not be disappointed at all.

"Cause I told you we might do more stuff later?"

"I...don't know what you mean."

"I think you do. But you see..." He walked towards me and stood still when his chest bumped against my breasts. "...I'm afraid I have to go now. You can shower here before you leave, though."

I wanted to tell him there was no point in showering cause I wasn't dirty from just sleeping, but I held my tongue. "I can shower in my own room. Where will you go?"

"That's not for you to know."

"Oh."

"I'd rather stick my tongue between your legs, though..." He said, breathing against my face.

"...!"

His hands suddenly grabbed my ass and he pulled my hips against his. If it wasn't for his hands on me, I would have laid flat on the ground like a puddle of mush. What the fuck was wrong with my knees when I was around this man? There was just something about him. I always thought people were born with such charisma but I knew that he wasn't born like that at all.

"How about you? Would you like that too? And for once, just be honest, woman."

His tongue between my legs, his lips sucking on my... Ok, I was gonna be honest. "Before our night, I hadn't got l-laid in almost half a year," I admitted. "So, I guess the answer is yes since I tend to be a little horny these days..."

"Half a year, huh? Fuck, that's long."

"Tell me about it."

"Why was it so long?" he asked, his lips already touching mine. He traced his tongue over my upper lip.

"I'm not a person to fuck around without a commitment." That sounded pretty stupid for someone who was working as a slave. I internally facepalmed.

"I have to admit that I like that. I wouldn't like it if you would sleep with just anybody," he said and I already opened my lips for him to have a taste. "But I gotta go now."

And he did.

"He didn't even finger you?" Bentley asked while she opened my fridge and got herself a drink. I guess we were basically living together in my house.

"No," I answered.

"You also didn't suck him off?"

"No."

"He also didn't lick your pussy?" Bentley asked, walking towards the couch. "Fuck you?"

"No." I sighed.

"Not even a little breast sucking?"

I glared at her. "No fingering, no sucking, no blowing, nothing. I said no sex at all, what's so hard to understand about that, girl?"

She gave me a glass of white wine too and sat next to me.

"I just don't understand. I know he fucked Cedi all the time. And I know he fucked you last time too. And if you would have been a bad fuck, I don't think that he would have chosen you over her..." Bentley seemed to think real hard. "Or have your skills gotten worse since we did a little bit of the naughty--"

"Please!" Why did she have to remind me of that again? "Don't bring that time up," I said. It was nice but it was way awkward too. "Anyway, it doesn't matter."

I gulped down a sip of wine.

"I guess. I just wondered, that's all..." She said. "So...wanna talk about something else? We're alone now anyway. "

She didn't need to explain what she wanted to talk about.

"Ok... I'll tell you everything."

Chapter 11

SPARTACUS

Mercedes opened the door. She looked at me, coldly, with those light green eyes of hers while she bit on the inside of her cheek. We still hadn't talked about the fact that she was now known as the dumped Rewarder instead of first choice.

"Morning, Cedi," I said, a little awkward.

"He's in the bathroom," she replied, turned her back to me, and walked into the room.

I nodded and walked inside as well, where I quickly rushed to the bathroom and found a hysterically crying—very naked—Crixus who was pacing in the bathroom.

With a gigantic erection.

"Jesus, fuck, man!" I cried out, looking at that huge black dick. It looked as fat as a beer can, I shit you not! And maybe he hadn't been lying when he bragged about those ten inches either.

I felt two emotions at the moment. Firstly, I felt pity—pity with all of Cedi's holes to be precise. And secondly, I felt kinda jealous. His was clearly way bigger than mine was. I knew I was being ridiculous because I had the most perfect cock myself and I knew flawlessly how to use it, but this one was certainly the winner when it came to size. I guess I was just a competitive type of guy.

He had called me when I was showering, half an hour ago. I was just in the middle of thinking about all the things I was gonna do to Tesla when I heard my phone ring. He shouted on the other side of the line that I needed to come straight away cause it was an emergency. This was certainly the last thing I expected to see.

"I'm sorry, man, that you have to witness...this," he cried, pointing at his third leg. "But I'm freaking out!" he yelled, stepping towards me.

"Look out, Crix, before you strike me down with that devil's breed!"

"I'm not handling jokes all too well now, man," he almost cried. "Just look at it!"

"Oh, trust me when I say it's impossible to not look at it. What's wrong?"

"I can't get it down and it hurts," he said, sweat gushing down his face. "I...I might have taken a pill or two too many...you know...just for some extra fun. But now it won't get soft and it's starting to itch like a bitch too. What do you think? Is that rash on the head there?"

I really didn't wanna inspect that thing but he seemed to be really worried.

"I guess it looks a little bumpy..." I admitted, looking at some purplish bumps.

"Oh my god!" he shouted, running around in the bathroom.

It was such a ridiculous sight to see.

"Crixus—"

"What must I do now? What if I can't ever use it again? I can't live that way, I need my dick! Oh, God! What if it falls off? What if—"

"Jesus, it won't fall off, but I'm no doctor," I answered. "It might shrink in size, though. Which wouldn't be such a bad thing..."

"Shut up, you!"

I laughed, but I also pitied my friend. "Maybe you should tell Gremelda so that she can call a doctor."

"No way. I don't want her to see my dick in this condition!"

"She doesn't have to see it, you dumbass. I'll tell her, ok?" I said, walking to the door. "It's either that or you might have to go through life...you know...dickless."

"Ok, fucking get her then," he sobbed.

When all the drama was solved, I returned to my empty room again. I dropped on the couch and watched some tv.

The doctor had given Crixus some other pills and he had to wait till his dick went soft again. He had luckily calmed down when the doctor said that there wouldn't be any long-term side effects. I was happy about that. God, only Crixus could end up in a situation like this. I don't think he'll ever take those pills again.

Madame Gremelda had been so fucking pissed.

There was nothing good on tv, so I turned it off again, grabbed my phone, and headed out to the bar.

I was bummed out that I had ordered Tesla to leave earlier. There were still six hours left until the twenty-four-hour policy was over. I also regretted I didn't fuck her last night. I just wanted to make her all desperate and horny and then take her in the morning. Morning sex had always been my favorite. But now Crixus had ruined it all with his pimpled horse dick episode!

She sat at the bar with Bentley. Hm, wasn't that girl usually Gannicus's Rewarder? Guess my buddy picked someone else yesterday.

I smiled and cocked my head at Tesla when I saw she noticed me, but my smile quickly vanished when I saw her puffy slightly red eyes.

Had she been crying? Wow, I guess she really wanted to get laid, but still, that was no reason to start crying, was it? I didn't like this, so I headed over to them.

"Hey," I said.

Bentley patted Tesla's shoulder and announced that she was gonna take a leak.

"What's wrong?" I asked as I sat on Bentley's stool. "You missed me that much, darling?"

Tesla scoffed but smiled at me. "Nothing's wrong. I was just...a bit emotional. You know, cause I miss my family."

I nodded. It was actually against the policies to talk about our past, so I didn't wanna get too involved, for her own sake.

"I understand," I said, patting her thigh. She looked at me through her long lashes. Jesus, look at those puppy eyes. I recognized a "fuck me cause I need you to comfort me badly" expression immediately when I saw one.

I smiled.. "You know...technically, you're still my Rewarder for the next few hours and I can't remember I dismissed you for the rest of the day...Do you remember such a thing?" I asked her.

She bit her lower lip and shook her head. "No, I don't recall you saying that to me. In fact, I think you said I was allowed to grab a drink at the bar and had to return to your room again..."

She grabbed her drink and gulped it down in one go.

"Yes, you're correct and I see you finished your drink. They say that it's good to drink before heavy exercise..." I said, wiggling my brows once.

"Yeah, I'm all done. So we will do some heavy exercise?"

"You got that right. This time, it'll be you who can get to work."

She took a big breath and nodded. "O-ok."

"Let's get the fuck out of here then," I said.

"Yes, Sir," Tesla replied as she stood up.

The last word spilling from her lips gave me some goosebumps at the back of my neck as I stood up too. We headed back to my bedroom with more than five hours left on the clock...

12

Chapter 12

TESLA

"Oh, fuck—" I panted as Spartacus pushed me against the wall.

While looking at me, he kicked his foot against the door, shutting it with a loud bang while his hands slipped underneath my dress. They were warm and rough to the touch.

He zipped open my dress and pushed it off my shoulders before he leaned in, breathed against the lace of my bra and sucked on one of my nipples through the thin fabric.

He kissed his way up until his mouth found mine, hungry lips devouring my lips as he unclasped my bra and took it off.

I desperately plucked the shirt out of his pants and pulled it over his head, hating to break the kiss in the process. His topless muscled chest instantly caused me to start drooling. God, his body was so damn hot!

During our last time, he was mostly the one in charge, but now I wanted it to be different, so I leaned in, and started kissing his neck, checking if I could make it a different experience now. I wanted to do some work too and at the bar, he said I could. I mean, if he didn't want it, he could tell me to stop or whatever, right? I was his for the next few hours, to do with as he pleased.

But he didn't say anything, except "fuck" when I pushed my hand inside his pants.

I sucked and licked from the right side of his neck to the left side, running my tongue over his Adam's apple and I felt him swallowing as his cock hardened in the palm of my hand. My tongue slid lower, over his chest and the hills of his eight-pack before I slithered higher again, sucking on one of his nipples. Fuck, I was so damn horny, my pussy wetting my panties.

He suddenly grabbed my ass and lifted me up like I was a weightless feather, walking us to the bed where he threw me onto the mattress.

"Take your panties off," he said with a hoarse voice. I followed his instruction.

After he'd pulled his own pants down, it was time for his underwear. I just threw my last piece of clothing to the floor and watched him take off his boxer briefs.

His beautiful hard-on flew out, smacked to his belly with a slap and I just wanted to dive between those strong powerful thighs.

"When you look at me like that, it's like you're begging for that mouth to be filled..." Spartacus said and I understood I was looking at him with my mouth hanging open.

This time I really was ogling him. And honestly, I wanted my mouth to be filled. It was fucking months ago since I sucked some dick and Spartacus's erection might be the very best specimen I'd ever seen.

He wrapped his hand around it and gave it a few tugs, making me almost choke on my own spit as I saw how he squeezed out a bead of clear liquid.

I kneeled and crawled on my hands and knees to the edge of the bed, towards him, and when I was close enough, I gave a long kitty-lick over his shimmering tip, tasting his pre-cum.

"Jesus," he breathed out while his hands fell on top of my head.

He looked at me, anticipation readable in his eyes, and I was happy to show this man why I was named the Queen of cocksucking by one of my exes.

I once more drew my tongue over his abs, left to right, while taking a comfortable position. When I sat comfortably, I dove down and took him into my mouth till his cock hit the back of my throat.

"Fuck," he gasped when I did it a few times more and then started sucking on the head, bobbing my head back and forth while one of my hands caressed his abs and the other his balls.

He had such a great cock and he smelled and tasted good too. I let my tongue roll over the rim, licked up and down the shaft, and deepthroated him some more while his hands were messing up my hair.

When a string of hair fell on my forehead and into my eyes, he softly brushed it away from my face. As I blinked up and my mouth was filled with his erection, I couldn't help to find that gesture cute somehow, the way he placed it so gently behind my ear while looking at me with dark eyes and an open mouth.

I couldn't get enough of him and as I was sucking him off like my life depended on it and slurping sounds bounced off the walls, he pushed me away from his cock, saliva dripping down my chin and a string of drool still connecting us before I wiped my mouth.

Oh, why did he do that?

"That's enough," he breathlessly ordered and grabbed my shoulders to push me on my back again. We kissed until it was him going down on me this time.

I felt his beard grazing down over my stomach and legs before he found his way to my most intimate spot. It felt so good, just like it had felt the last time. That soft tongue and that coarse beard, tickling me everywhere.

He started licking my swollen lips, taking them in his mouth and gently sucking on them, drool dripping down my hole while he played with my pussy as he pleased.

Breathing heavily, I threw my head back when he started licking and sucking on my clit and pushed a few fingers inside at the same time.

I almost went crazy by what he was doing to me for minutes, until he stopped it all and crawled back up, rolling us around, and sat up. He leaned back against the headboard and I straddled him and lowered my hips, impaling myself with him till he was buried all the way inside. Fuck, I just loved that we didn't need to use condoms because we were all medically tested and I'm on the pill anyway.

I grabbed the headboard with both hands to secure myself. And now, I was gonna do my Invicta name some honor and show him how I could be a good ride.

He leaned in and kissed me as my hips were bobbing up and down, his dick grazing over my g-spot like it was specially made and curved for it. It hit me exactly where it should. "Ahh!" I moaned in his mouth when his hands grabbed my ass cheeks and moved with me at the same pace, supporting me as they squeezed.

When I opened my eyes for a moment, I saw he watched me in action. I didn't mind it, in fact, it only turned me on more.

At some point, when little beads of sweat started to roll down his forehead, Spartacus started to rub my clit in the process. It felt so good. I didn't wanna come so soon but on the other hand I wanted it now.

When he also sucked on my tits, I was too far gone to hold back.

"I'm coming," I cried out and fell apart in pure bliss, clenching all around his cock. "Ahh...shit!" I moaned, fucking him hard as I rode out my high. His fingers rubbed my clit through my orgasm and somewhere in the background, I heard him curse as he climaxed too.

I laid my head down on his chest, panting breathlessly from the intensive exercise.

"Damn..." He said. "Were you that desperate, darling?"

I chuckled, dead-tired but so satisfied. "What is it with you calling me darling?" I mumbled.

"I just like it," he said as he slowly caressed my back.

"Do you call everyone your darling when they're with you?"

"Mostly."

"Well, now I feel less special," I replied.

"You are special, though..."

I looked up and he gazed at me with an expression in his eyes which was exactly like he had when I knew him as Dean. It was hard to recognize him in the beginning, but the more I saw him, the more I felt stupid for not seeing it straight away.

And every time I did, I felt guilty all over again.

After I laid my head on his chest again, he asked, "if we were to meet outside of the hotel, and I would ask you out, would you say yes this time?"

"I don't wanna answer that," I answered.

"Oh, why not?" he softly asked while his hand started stroking my spine again.

"Because if I say yes, that makes me an even bigger hypocrite bitch."

I didn't want you then but now you're hot so I do want you now. I didn't want to think like that...

"And if you say no?" he asked.

"Then that would make me a liar, I suppose."

"So, you want to say yes?"

"What does it matter? We're here, not somewhere else, and we can't date while we're here anyway. That's what Shana—I mean Bentley has told me."

Spartacus took a big breath and sighed. "I know. There's a reason for it too."

"What's that?"

"How would it make you feel if we were together and I picked another Rewarder as my prize?" he asked.

"I'd cut your balls off."

"Well, look at it the other way around. What if I would lose and the winner picks you? You can't refuse because you don't want him, and I can't forbid him to pick you. I mean I probably will try to forbid him, but he doesn't need to listen to me."

"But you always win anyway..." I said, rather proudly of him.

I sat up straight and looked at him.

"That's true." He smirked. "But you never know. Maybe by some miracle, someone else wins on one of their lucky evenings."

I slowly got off of him, making his soft dick slide out, followed by his cum. "What would you do now then? If someone else would pick me?" I asked.

I couldn't bear the thought of having sex with another guy. I just didn't wanna. I wouldn't say I was in love with Spartacus now, and I knew he wasn't in love with me. Why would he be? I was a total bitch to him. I don't even get why he chose me again. I mean, the first time he was clearly punishing me, but he chose me again... I was happy, though. He was an amazing guy. Maybe I wasn't in love, but I did like him. He was hard not to like. He's hot, sweet, and funny.

"I wouldn't let that happen," he answered.

"But you just said that if by some miracle someone might win—"

"It simply will not happen," he said and walked to the bathroom. "Come with me," he said, turning around and making a come here finger gesture.

"Yes, Sir." I smiled.

13

Chapter 13

Spartacus

"Tomorrow will be ein fery schpecial day to all of us," Gremelda said as she walked at an excruciatingly slow pace in front of us while we all stood in a line next to each other. I swear, sometimes she made me feel like this was some sort of detention camp or whatever.

"Und you all will behave at zee fery best, or I'll be fery displeased." She stopped in front of me and breathed into my face. "We wouldn't want zat, now would we, Spartacus?"

"No, ma'am," I answered.

I wondered what would be so special for her to summon up her whole team. Gladiators and Rewarders, the team that handled the bets, and Oenomaus were all present.

"Would you like to know why tomorrow is ein schpecial day?" she asked, walking to the next man in line, Gannicus.

"I would, oh, very beautiful Madame Gremelda," he answered.

Oh my God, What a suckup was that man.

"Tomorrow," she continued, walking to the line of Rewarders, and I couldn't help but to look at Tesla instead of looking at her. "We will get a fery schpecial visitor."

Tesla's eyes found mine but I wished they hadn't because Gremelda stopped in front of her, grabbed her chin, and yanked her face in her direction. She immediately looked at the German lady, eyes wide with fear.

"Tomorrow, zee boss of all Invicta hotels will pay us a vizit to inspect our hotel. You people all know mein hunger for competitiveness. Und if you don't know, then you do now," she said, releasing poor Tesla. "I want our boss to see that we are zee best. We have an impeccable reputation and zis Invicta earns zee best money out of all other hotels in zee world. Tomorrow, we will show him how we work and why we are zee best and I want NO mistakes. I want zee best show tomorrow!" She walked towards the door. "Meeting ist over," she said and left.

"Jesus, I'm so afraid of that woman," Crixus said.

"I'm not. I love that woman," Gannicus replied, standing between Crixus and me while wrapping his arms around our shoulders as we walked to the arena for training again. "She's so cute with that German accent. Especially when she's all angry and shouting all these German words like 'nein' or 'du hurensohn'. I have no idea what the fuck it means, but it's precious."

"Hurensohn means son of a whore, you dumbass, it's not meant to be precious at all." Cedi sighed as she walked past us.

"Oh, hey, Cedi," Crixus said with the sweetest voice ever used.

I looked over my shoulder and found Tesla's eyes again. She was just wiping some sweat off of her forehead which she no doubt got from Gremelda's action. Her cheeks were all red from where Gremelda had grabbed her. Poor girl. I smiled at her with sympathy. We all had to undergo Gremelda's treatment on some day.

She waved me goodbye when she and the other Rewarders went in different directions from us Gladiators.

"How is someone like Gremelda cute?" Crixus asked.

"What can I say, in my dreams, I'm making her mine."

"Well, dream on," I told Gannicus. "It's not allowed, but even if it was, Gremelda would never hook up with a swine like you. She has a certain grace, she has class. And you? My dear Gannicus, you are proud to fart and burp at the same time." I rolled my eyes.

"Hey, that's not easy, man!" he replied.

"You stand zero chance with her, buddy."

The boss had arrived this afternoon, so, just like Gremelda had ordered, we were to give him a "fery schpecial" show. She really went all the way because before we were up, there were all these exotic dancers performing some freaky magical fire dancing show. It was quite spectacular and I wondered if the Boss would be impressed with what we had to offer after this sensation. Maybe she dug her own grave with this.

While I waited backstage in the arena, I saw her sitting next to a man I'd never seen before. He had to be the big boss, but he seemed so much younger than I expected him to be. Maybe it was just because I couldn't see him clearly.

"You think that's him?" Crixus asked.

"I think so."

"He looks so young."

"I was thinking the exact same thing," I replied.

"He must be so loaded," Crixus said. "And scary."

"Fucking loaded." He didn't look so scary though. But I knew he was, he was the boss of all and this was a scary world. Our guests weren't just any kind of men. They were murderers, hitmen, psychopaths, and more, and he was the one that had to control them.

Because we had to please Gremelda, Oenomaus decided we did the blind battles tonight. Guess who was one of the gladiators wearing one? Honestly, I was so not in the mood for that. Not that I ever was, but ok.Luckily, everything went well. I obviously won and currently, I was being inspected and observed by no one other than the boss, who stood in front of me, his eyes tracing all over my body.

He was indeed young. But there was something else about him. He had a certain air that made me feel smaller than I actually was. Maybe it was just his status, I don't know. It was a feeling.

"I have to say that it was rather spectacular to see my employees in action and I fully understand why this hotel is so successful when it comes to gladiator gambling. Other hotels can learn from you fine gentleman," he said, walking back to stand next to Gremelda, who looked as proud as can be.

"Zank you, Sir," Gremelda said.

"I can see why the men are so eager to battle and win. The prices aren't nothing. Gremelda, your collection of Rewarders is remarkable. What a bunch of beauties together before me."

"I am fery pleased myself."

He walked to the line of Rewarders and something just didn't feel right. I had an uneasy feeling. Especially when he stopped before Tesla a little longer than he stood before the rest of them.

"So, normally they pick their prizes now?" he asked.

"Yes, Sir."

"Call me William. All that Sir all the time makes me feel so old."

"Fery well, William."

If I wouldn't know any better, I would dare to say that Gremelda actually seemed capable of blushing. I knew she'd never admitted to it, though.

I can't blame her. Boss was actually quite an attractive young man. He was dressed in a suit made to fit his body like a glove. You could just see he reeked of money. His hair was quite long but cut as if he just stepped out of a fashion magazine. It was light brown with a few blonde streaks. He had a little bit of a tan. His jawline almost killed me and his eyes were brown but so light. I'd never seen that before.

"Spartacus is to pick first because he won, right?" he asked.

"Yes, he ist," Gremelda answered.

William looked at me again. "So, who would you pick today?"

"Uhh...I would pick Tesla," I answered.

"Oh, why?"

"Because...she's cute?" I said, and it somehow came out as a question.

I mean, what was I supposed to say? I couldn't tell I knew her as Ryah. I couldn't tell I liked her. I couldn't tell she simply just belonged to me and me alone.

"She certainly is." William agreed. "Well, gentlemen and miladies, I won't hold you up any longer. You can claim your prizes," he said, walking to the door. Gremelda followed him like a bitch. "You don't have to keep me company from now on, Gremelda. You have certainly proved yourself," he added.

"O-oh, yes. Zank you, William."

He then opened the door but stopped his motions. "However..." The hairs on my neck stood up straight when the uneasy feeling came back to me again. And I was right. "I'm afraid that Spartacus has to pick someone else tonight. Tesla, follow me, please."

Tesla looked at me briefly, biting her lip before she nervously walked towards William.

I wanted to stop them. I wanted to shout at the boss that he should go fuck himself, but I couldn't.

Fuck!

14

Chapter 14

TESLA

William guided me to some place in the hotel I had never been before. A floor where only the most important people stayed.

He beeped open one of the doors and pointed inside, a motion for me to get in before him, which I did without question.

It was an office and after I had stepped inside, I didn't dare to look, but I knew he stood right behind me. God knows what he was doing. Checking me out? Smelling my hair? Getting a cord out of his pocket to strangle me to death? Ok, I don't know where that came from, but I really didn't feel at ease around this man. Why did he want me to come along with him? He was at the top of the Invicta chain where I was just a mere new employee. I was nothing.

He closed the door and walked past me and I couldn't help but notice how his cologne smelled nice. After he sat down on his chair, he told me to sit on the chair opposite his desk, so I did.

"So...Tesla," he started. "Tell me about yourself."

"Uh...what would you like to know?"

"Whatever you wanna tell me. Tell me what you did before you came to work for me."

"I'm not good at that sorta stuff--introducing myself I mean...and Gremelda told us that we are forbidden to speak about life before Invicta..."

William laughed and looked at me with twinkling eyes. "Is Gremelda the one calling the shots here or am I that person?"

"Oh, you of course. I...I d-didn't mean that--"

"It's ok, Tesla. How about I tell you something about myself first?" he asked while tapping a few fingers against the desk top.

"Oh, ok, y-yeah, sure," I stuttered.

"I'm William, twenty-eight years old and an absolute fan of anything that has to do with cooking and food. Do you have a passion for that? Cooking and food?"

Ok, didn't expect that he was going to talk about food. "Yeah, I do." Everybody likes food, right?

"How about Polish food?" he asked.

"Polish...food?"

Thinking about that country and food in one sentence took me back to that fateful night--the night that got me into the whole mess. The reason I have to stay here because jail or death would be my only other option.

"Yeah, Polish food. I thought you liked that, cause...a little birdie told me you did," William said.

"..."

I swallowed. Did he know what happened that day? How could he?

"Oh, yeah, I know all about you, Ryah," he said as if he was reading my mind.

"B-but--"

"I know everything about everyone. And Ramone, the one that ended up dead? That was my cousin."

My eyes grew large at what he just told me.

"Oh, come on Ryah," Jason whined.

"No, man," I said.

He followed me through my apartment, asking me the same stupid question over and over again, like a child that wouldn't take no for an answer. He wanted me to participate in one of his stupid illegal activities again. I didn't wanna do those things anymore.

"I'll pay you double, come on. You only have to take that guy to that Polish restaurant. He's got the hots for slutty girls, so I'm sure he wanna fuck you."

I punched him on his nose, making him fall to his knees and grunt out loud. "Asshole."

"Ok, fuck, I think you just broke my nose. Ok...ok, I shouldn't have called you a slut again. But come on, 500 bucks. You only have to take him out and maybe have sex with him if he wanna. That's it. Didn't you whine it's been a while since you got laid? This is a win-win. I heard he's hot."

"I'm not a prostitute," I said.

"Whatever, it's just sex, woman."

I hated to admit it but I could use the money... "Why a Polish restaurant?" I asked. Not that it was that important but I just think it's an odd choice to pick. I mean Italian, sure. Greek, great. French, of course. But why Polish?

"Cause the guy's mother was from there and he has a mommy complex so he is a bit obsessed with that country."

"Oh-kay..."

"So you'll do it?"

"I didn't say that."

"But you will, right?"

I sighed. "Fine."

I could definitely use the money after my boss kicked me out two months ago.

Ramone wasn't only good-looking, he was funny and kind and smart. And a policeman too. I wondered why I had to take him out to dinner since he appeared to be quite the catch. Maybe I even thought about going out on a second date with him! I certainly thought about asking him to come for a "coffee" later at my place. Jason was right, this was a win-win. Ramone was great.

"I have to say, Ryah, I think you're the most gorgeous lady I've ever been on a date with," Ramone praised.

"Thank you. You're not too bad yourself."

"Actually, I am."

"Hm?"

"I am a bad man. And I really like you, that's why I'm gonna have to ask you to leave this restaurant while I stay behind," he said. "And believe me when I say I'm asking you that with pain in my heart."

We didn't even have the main course yet. And I meant the actual main course--the food not the sex. What was he talking about? "But...we aren't done here...?"

"We are done."

"But--"

"I know you've been asked to go out on this date with me. And it's because I like you, I'm telling you to leave."

"Uh...ok."

I was so disappointed, but he persuaded me to do what he said.

The day after, my aunt asked me if I could visit her. She lived on the other side of town. Since I had nothing more important to do and was still a bit bummed out about last night, I went.

It was there, where I heard on the news that a cop was killed. When I saw his photo and his name, I was flabbergasted and the most strange uneasy feeling came over me. His name was Ramone. It was "my" policeman Ramone.

It somehow felt as if I had lured him to that restaurant, where he was found dead on the toilet.

"Ramone was your cousin?"

"He was," William said as he loosened his tie and took it off. "He actually was a cop for real. But he was sort of a dirty cop, if you know what I mean. Me and my family, we don't really care about the law and all that. We, however, care about our family a lot..."

"I swear to God, I had n-nothing to do with any of this. I-I actually liked him, b-but he told me to leave, I don't know why he wanted me to leave b-but he said I should."

Oh, God, was William going to kill me now? How would he do it? Shoot me in the head? Strangle me with that cord? Rip out my beating heart?

"This hotel is against violence, remember?" he said. "I won't do anything to you since I am a firm believer of following my own rules. But I do need you to tell me everything you know. If you do that, I promise you are completely safe here in this hotel. A lot safer than you would be when you were outside. Cause it's not only the police that searches for you, but it's also the underworld. It's a shitshow your buddy Jason pulled you into."

"W-why?" Why would they? I didn't do anything. What could I have done to a cop/mafia family member? I was just one person. "Where's Jason?"

"Don't you worry about him..."

"O-ok." I couldn't help but worry, though.

As I started biting my nails, William opened one of his drawers and took out a bottle of liquor. He poured it in two glasses and by the time he was done, I had bitten my skin so much, I tasted blood.

He shoved one of the glasses in my direction. "Now tell me everything you know."

15

Chapter 15

SPARTACUS

Because Tesla was taken from me by that fuckface William, I chose Bentley as my Rewarder tonight. I couldn't pick Cedi anymore because I didn't wanna anger Crixus and I also just didn't feel the need to fuck anyone else but Tesla. Basically, I didn't care who would be my Rewarder at all.

"What do you think he'll do to her?" Bentley asked me while nervously bouncing her leg up and down.

"I don't know," I said for the nth time.

We actually sat in Tesla's apartment at the moment because Bentley had a key.

"I hope she's not in trouble," she said, biting her lip.

"Wait, is there a reason you say it like that? Why would she be in trouble?" I asked.

"..."

"Bentley?"

"Nothing. You're right, she didn't do anything wrong. I'm just finding it odd that she had to go with William. I mean, she's hot, can't deny that, but why only Tesla?"

"I don't know and you're making me nervous with the way you're acting," I said as I sat down next to the girl on the couch.

"Sorry," she apologized.

"Nothing is going on with her or anything, is there?" I asked, suddenly more worried than before.

"No...no, man."

I didn't know if I believed that. "Cause you should tell me if there is."

"Why?"

"What why?"

"Why should I tell you? You have nothing to do with her. She's your Rewarder if you need her to be and that's it," she suddenly snapped.

"Jesus, fuck, woman."

She opened her mouth to say something in return, but we all of a sudden heard some loud giggles outside and the door beeped open. In came Tesla.

In came a very drunk Tesla.

"Oh, hey, buddies!" She said, smiling with red cheeks.

Bentley walked over to her and Tesla fell against her, face to shoulder, almost making them both fall to the floor. I rushed over and held Tesla in my arms to stop her from tripping while Bentley closed the door.

"What the fuck did he give you to become this drunk in just a short while?" Bentley asked.

I was fuming inside. Bentley was right. What had William done with her? Tesla's hair was all ruffled up, the top button of her dress was open and her lipstick was all smudged

"Oh, just a few g-glasses of some fucking expensive liquor I don't know the name of. It burned in m-my throat, haha," she hiccuped.

"But S-shana, you should leave," she said, wiggling herself out of my arms and turning to her friend to push Bentley towards the door. "Cause... I'm gonna suck D-dean's cock and I don't want you to s-see my s-skills cause you might get jealous I'm way better than you--" She burped. "You'll be jous...I mean Jea-lous. Yeah, you may become j-jealous, girl."

Bentley didn't seem to be surprised that Tesla had called me Dean, so I figured she probably knew we had a past. I also felt they did too.

Bentley sighed. "Tesla--"

"Get out!"

"What the fuck, when did you become this strong?" Bentley asked.

"Get out, let me suck cock!"

"Ok, ok, Jesus." Bentley looked at me with glaring eyes as she let herself get pushed out, probably because she didn't want Tesla to make a scene. "Bring her to bed," she told me, though it was more of a warning.

I nodded. "I will." As if she had to be afraid that I was the kind of man who would bang a drunk woman. No, thanks.

Tesla closed the door. "What? Bed? But I don't wanna go to bed...I w-wanna cock some suck." She burst out in laughter. "I mean I wanna sock some cuck. Wait, that's not right either. H-help me, Dean," she whined, clutching at my shoulders. "I want you in my m-mouth. I owe you, cause...cause I've been a bitch t-to you when we were young."

"You should go to bed."

"But...don't you want me?" She looked at me, licking her lips.

"I want you," I answered while I picked her up, bridal style. "But not if you're wasted like this."

"But why do you still want me? I've...I've been such a huge bitch to you."

"You should sleep, darling."

I laid her in bed and helped her take off her clothes. Actually, it was more me that undressed her. "You're s-so sweet," she whispered, her eyes already closing, but her hands still running through my hair as I took off her stockings.

"I know," I replied.

When I was done, I looked at her. She was already snoring so I pulled the sheets over her body. She looked so cute with her blushing red apple cheeks and a little smile on her face.

I sighed and laid down next to her. Fuck it if someone would find out we spent the night together.

"Oh, shit..."

I heard someone waking me up with a hoarse voice. "Morning, sunshine," I answered.

"Shit."

I sat up and next to me, Tesla also sat up straight, her hands on top of her head.

"Headache?"

"Shit fuck."

"Yeah, you had a little too much to drink, darling." I rubbed her back.

"I can't even remember how I came home," she said.

"You came home, pushed Bentley out, wanted to suck my cock, pouted when I said you weren't allowed and then you fell asleep." I summoned it up for her in one sentence.

"Jeez. I'm so sorry."

"It was mostly funny," I responded, wanting to ask what happened yesterday but I figured out she wasn't fully awake yet so I held my tongue.

She kicked away the sheets and stood up before she waddled out of the room. "Gotta go to the bathroom."

A moment later, we sat at her table, eating breakfast. She didn't want to eat but I told her that she should because of her hangover, that it would help, so now, she nibbled on a cracker.

"What happened?" I casually asked. "With William, I mean..."

She sighed. "We...talked. And later, he wanted to fuck me."

I swear, I almost choked on my milk. "Did you let him?"

"I felt I had no choice..."

"...!"

I know it wasn't my place to get emotional about this. Tesla wasn't mine, but I was so fucking agitated about this. Like really, really fucking agitated. I slammed my glass of milk on the table.

"But I didn't allow him," she then said.

"Huh?" I blinked up at her.

"It was scary though. He's like the boss of, you know...the underworld and all that stuff. But he told me in our conversation before that he loved his own rules. So when he made a move on me, I said no to him. He asked me how I dared to go against him and I said he wasn't a Gladiator. In my contract, it said that I'm hired to offer my services to the Gladiators. His rules." She nibbled on his cracker, taking a few bites before she threw the thing on the plate. "I can't eat anymore."

"So...what did he say when you refused?" I asked.

"He was acting really weird," Tesla replied. "He laughed out loud and told me how wonderful I was. That I was right and that nobody had ever refused him. "

"Why...why didn't you want it, though? I mean, the guy's hot..."

"Yeah, I guess... But, I dunno. I just didn't want to sleep with him." She shrugged.

I smiled and took a big bite of my egg sandwich. I was happy again. She didn't want William but she wanted me yesterday.

"You want a bite?" I asked, holding a piece of egg to her nose.

"Fuck, no. The smell alone makes me wanna gag. Shit, twenty-five and I can't even take it anymore to be drunk just for one night," she complained, rubbing over her face with both of her hands.

"So, how about that blowjob then?" I asked.

"No thanks," she replied, mumbling behind her hands.

"No? But you were the one wanting to give me one, remember?" I said, chuckling.

"No, thanks."

"I like you when you're moody."

"No thanks."

She looked at me through her fingers and I laughed. "Are you ashamed now for the way you behaved yesterday?"

"No, because thankfully I can't remember much about yesterday, apart from my time at William's office. After that, it's all gone."

"Hm. I'm offended that you remember him, but not me. I was a gentleman and didn't take advantage of you."

She took a sip of tea. "I'm very thankful."

"Good...so, uh, I gotta go soon," I said, leaning in to wipe away a piece of cracker that was stuck to the corner of her mouth.

"You h-have to?" she asked, her breath hitching at our touch.

"Yeah, can't stay."

"But you and the others don't have training today, do you?"

"The ones that don't have a Rewarder, do have training. I picked Bentley, but I'm not using her anyway so I think I'll train today. Besides that, we aren't allowed to hang out..."

I was bummed out about that but also really wanted to check up on my brother. Something I hadn't done last night.

"Ok...well...maybe we'll see each other at the restaurant tonight?" she asked.

I smiled at her and she smiled at me. It was amazing that it felt so natural. The thought I would see her again tonight made me so happy. "I hope we will."

16

Chapter 16

TESLA

It mortified me, thinking of how I behaved like a fool last night. This morning, I told Spartacus that I could hardly recall what had happened in my hotel room, but the truth was that I remembered some of it. It's not that I remembered it all, but I had gotten some flashbacks here and there before he asked me.

"Oh, God. I begged him for his cock," I whispered to myself before I buried my face in the pillow that laid on the couch. "I literally begged him."

It was so humiliating.

He must think of me as a joke now. My embarrassing evening of begging for a penis between my lips wasn't the worst of my troubles, though.

I recalled the talk I had with my boss.

"Oh, God, what must I do now?" I asked, already panicking.

The idea that not only the police but also the underworld was searching for me was pretty terrifying. I didn't know that Ramone was a dirty cop. He seemed so nice and cool and sweet. Maybe he was all that, but he came from a criminal family too, who, apparently, wanted to know all I had got to say about my evening with him. The last evening of his life.

I had provided William with all the information I could think of, and I cursed Jason in my mind for involving me in all of this shit.

However, I also was afraid of what they were going to do to him. Jason wasn't exactly my friend or anything like that, he was more a guy who sometimes needed my help and I, in exchange, needed cash, which I got if I helped him. That was pretty much it. But I still didn't want him to get slaughtered, and I certainly didn't want to get slaughtered myself for just dining with a hot dude.

I guess I'd been stupid. I should have known there was something up with what he asked of me. Why would I get paid a few hundred bucks just to go to dinner with a great guy? I feel they used me to distract him or something. Or was I just his type?

"You don't have to worry," William answered. "I believe what you just told me and I'm often able to tell if people are lying to me."

"Ok." Somehow, I believed him too, and I didn't feel unsafe with him. He seemed to be one of those criminals that was honorable, like the ones you always see in shows. That dude from the Blacklist, he's a criminal but a good honorable one, William was like that. Please let William be like that!

I had no other choice but to believe that. I bit my lip and sighed again before I grabbed my glass to gulp down the alcohol he just poured in a glass for me. "Fuck me, that b-burns," I said in a hoarse voice. Jesus!

"Yeah, it's pretty strong," William replied, wearing a smirk on his face.

"No shit?" I answered.

"Another one?" he asked after he drank his glass empty too—with much more grace than I did—and filled it again.

"Please." I nodded. I was still nervous as fuck. "And I'm sorry I just said shit and fuck."

William laughed while running a hand through his hair after some had fallen to the front. I had to admit that he was a pretty damn hot man, but not as hot as Spartacus was.

He refilled my glass and after he put the bottle away, he said, "You didn't say fuck. You said fuck me..."

I swallowed. "I—I don't know...did I?"

He ran his tongue over his lower lip and hummed. "Hmm-hmm..."

"...!"

I quickly finished my drink and coughed because I was too hasty for my own good.

William stood up, walked around his desk, and patted my back until I was done coughing. He then leaned in till I felt his lips brushing against my ear. His touch made my breath hitch.

"Would you like me to fuck you, then? Or do you prefer to ride my dick?" he asked. "Hm?"

"Uh..." I almost choked on my saliva.

It was then and there that I'd blurted out that I'm only there to serve the Gladiators, that it thrilled me that he helped me out, but that I couldn't sleep with him because it was against the rules. I'd been so afraid that he would get angry, but he laughed out loud instead. We drank some more until I think it was him who said that I wasn't getting another refill and I needed to get the fuck out of his office.

The sound of my door that opened snapped me out of my thoughts. I looked up. It was Bentley.

"Well, well, well... Look who's all sober again," she said, slamming the door. My head throbbed at the loud sound. "You look like shit."

"I feel like shit too," I answered.

"What happened yesterday? Did the boss try anything weird?"

"No... He...he knows what's happened."

Bentley first walked to my fridge and took out a drink. Why did she always come here to eat and drink first thing? She looked at me with a beer in her hand, and I shook my head in reply. I wasn't in the mood to drink. In fact, I'll never drink again.

I laid my head back against the couch, closing my eyes.

"You mean he knows what happened with that cop?"

I nodded.

"How?"

"Cause Ramone was part of his family." Bentley spat out her gulp of beer. Practically showering me by doing so. "Jeez, woman," I whined, drying my arm against her shirt.

She frowned. "Do you think he knew about this before Invicta hired you?"

"Huh?"

"Do you think he knew it was you before he looked into your file? I mean...it was Gremelda that asked me—and specifically me, not the other Rewarders—if I knew a hot, handsome, smart lady who could become our next Rewarder. Obviously, I dropped your name."

"She only asked you?" She nodded. I thought about it, but it made no sense. "But why didn't William just pay me a visit at my house if he already knew who I was even before I started working here?"

"I don't know. I'm just saying it's a coincidence. Isn't it?"

I scratched my head. I wasn't in my right mind to think about all this. "I don't know...But I guess it doesn't matter anyway. He told me I had nothing to worry about, that he would fix things."

"And you believe him?" Bentley asked, bouncing a leg up and down. She always did that when she was nervous. I laid my hand on her leg, stopping her movements.

"I have no fucking idea who killed Ramone or why he got killed. I don't know why I got involved in all this mess, either. I just know I have a headache right now." I sighed. "Don't worry, ok? I'm here now, and I'm safe."

She took a big breath. "Ok."

I ran my hand through her hair. "It's so long," I said.

"Yeah... There are a few Gladiators who dig super long hair, so."

"Who's your favorite?" I asked.

"I don't really have one. I'm mostly picked by Gannicus, so he's familiar and he's funny. I don't mind him."

"Good fucker?" I asked.

"Yeah, he is. But we don't always do it."

"Really?" I asked before I laid my head on her shoulder. "I wouldn't have guessed that from the few times I've briefly seen him. That he wouldn't grasp every opportunity to fuck someone, I mean."

"Oh, he's a sensitive one. He has a big mouth, but he's very emotional and all that. He cried like a baby a few times, talking about how he hadn't found his true love yet."

"Ahh, poor guy." I closed my eyes. "Are we allowed to gossip about them like this?"

"Well, the contract doesn't forbid gossiping. And it's not like Spartacus is standing behind our back, hearing how he's insulted to the core." I slapped her legs. Like, really hard. "Ouch!" she cried out.

"You know how bad I feel about that. You don't have to make it worse."

"Jesus Christ, girl. It happened, you feel bad, you said sorry, he forgave you. Let it go." She rubbed over her legs and I hoped she was in severe pain. "Ok, I shouldn't have teased you," she continued. "But it's not like you're a bad person. Do you think other people never say bad things about others? They do. You were just so dumb to get caught while you were in the middle of doing it. But believe me, there's no human in this world who hasn't insulted someone behind their backs in some way."

I sighed. "Maybe."

"Not maybe. I'm just right. Like, everybody is so into body positivity and all that, but if they see a fat girl walking around in a miniskirt, they gossip behind the girl's back about how her legs looked so hideous, showing all those gross dimples and cellulite. Oh, how dare she walk around like that while she has that size? That fucking pig. Ugh, bitches! And then they pretend everyone is so beautiful and beauty is all within." She made a gagging sound.

I couldn't help but laugh at her rant. "This feels like the good old days."

"Yeah, I've missed us."

"Me too."

"So, will you stop already? You won't burn in hell because you said something bad when you were sixteen."

"I was seventeen."

"Whatever. You know what I mean and you know I'm right," she said.

"You're always right."

"I know. We should all just try to be a little nicer and less judgmental about others. Luckily, we learn from our mistakes," she said wisely before she took a sip of beer.

"Hmm-hmm," I hummed.

"By the way, Mahindra has the tiniest baby-dick if you compare it with Crixus's."

I guess wise Bentley didn't last for very long.

17

CHAPTER 17

SPARTACUS

Fuck.

Getting out of bed had been a disaster this morning, but right now it felt like I could barely keep standing on my jelly-like legs. My head hurt. I felt a burn behind my watery eyes, and my teeth chattered like I was outside at zero degrees with no clothes on. I felt cold, yet hot.

"Spartacus!" Oenamous's voice echoed through the underground hall.

"Y-yes," I said as I looked up at him.

"Where are you? Cause you sure as hell aren't paying attention right here." His angry frown faded before he walked over to me and touched my forehead. "Jesus. I think you have a fever. Get back to your room right now, I'll inform Gremelda so that she can send someone to check up on you."

I didn't want to go back to my room or have someone to check up on me. All I wanted was to fight tonight. "No, I can--" I cut myself off with a long cough.

"No discussion," Oenamous said when I was done coughing like a seal. "I know you love a good match, but I can't let you fight in this condition. You're a fool for coming here in the first place. Go to your room and get the fuck in bed." He then ordered Crixus to guide me to my place and put me to bed.

The moment Oenamous had said he knew I loved a good match was the moment I realized it wasn't about fighting at all. It was about winning, and not because I wanted to be the best. It was because the idea that another Gladiator would pick Tesla as a Rewarder instead of me was something I just could not let happen.

When I didn't immediately move, Oenamous got irritated, so I left. But it was mostly because it felt like I was almost going to faint.

I debated what I should do when Crixus helped me to bed. Should I ask for his help or not? While he fetched me a glass of water and closed the curtains, I had a discussion with myself.

"You gotta help me," I said breathlessly, after I decided.

"What is it? Are you in pain? Do you want a painkiller?"

I shook my head. "No, I need your help with something else. You gotta win this evening."

"Dude, I'm number two, and you, the number one, aren't there. Of course, I'm going to win."

"And you'll have to pick Tesla when you do."

"Uhh...no? I'm going to pick Cedi."

Damn it, I totally forgot about Cedi! Surely, he wouldn't pick the one I wanted to prevent from sleeping with others over the one he wanted to prevent from sleeping with others.

"Fuck!" I cursed and grabbed my head. This didn't do my headache any favor.

Why did I have to become sick today? I haven't been sick in like, four years. Now, when finally the first match came after the last match's disaster where I didn't get to take Tesla to my room because of that twat William, I was fucking sick!

Crixus looked at me with confused eyes. "Why would you want me to--"

"Ok, change of plans. Gannicus will win and will pick Tesla. Sorry, but you'll have to lose. But if he does anything to that girl, I'll fucking end him. "

"Jesus!" Crixus cried out, pointing his finger at my face. If I had more strength, I would slap it away cause, God, that was annoying. "You like her, don't you?" he asked.

"..."

"You know the rules--"

"Yeah, well, fuck the rules."

"Spartacus!"

"Listen, you might have watched all these months how I fucked Cedi because you did nothing about it, but I won't let that happen. All you had to do was tell me how much you liked her and I would have picked another, Crix. I didn't know you had feelings for her. But...yeah, I like Tesla and I don't want the others to have her."

He furrowed his eyebrows, looking a tad sad suddenly. "But it's against the rules," he said in a soft voice.

"Are you going to tell on me? Will Gannicus?"

He shook his head. "Of course I won't, and I don't think Gannicus will. I trust that guy with my life, but Gremelda isn't stupid. She'll--"

"That's a worry for later. Will you do it? I know it's a lot to ask, I know how badly you want to win, but--" I took a breath, being all dizzy. "I'll let you win from me in a later match."

"I don't want to win like that, Spart."

"Please?"

Crixus already opened his mouth to give me an answer, but closed it when a knock on the door came, followed by a beep. Gremelda opened it and entered with a physician. "Leave," she ordered Crixus. I'm sure it bummed her out that her best fighter laid in bed like a pathetic, useless thing.

I looked at Crixus and he nodded at me as he headed out, making me feel relieved, knowing he just agreed to my proposal.

After a checkup, I was told I had to take rest, drink plenty of liquids, and had to sweat it out. Gremelda took the doctor's advice very seriously and called the cook to make me some broth before she tucked me in like I was a little sick child, a wet washcloth on my forehead and all that. I had to admit it was nice being pampered. If only it would be someone else who did the pampering...

Gentle hands brushed through my hair, waking me up. The touch felt amazing. Maybe it was because I felt a little high from being ill, I don't know, but it felt so relaxing. After I opened my eyes, it was revealed that the hands belonged to Tesla. Was my fever so high that I was hallucinating or something?

"Oh, I'm sorry. I didn't mean to wake you," she said, pulling her hand away.

"No," I all but cried out. "Caress me again," I ordered. She obliged. "Shouldn't you be with Gannicus?"

"Gannicus?" she asked, while stroking my hair at a soft pace.

I closed my eyes again, relishing the feeling. "Yeah. Didn't he win and pick you?"

"I don't know. Gremelda asked if one of us wanted to volunteer to stay with and take care of you, and I beat the other Rewarders by calling dibs. I've been here for hours. You slept this whole time."

She was here for hours already? "My lucky day," I replied, smiling. I guess I didn't need my plan after all.

"Can I get you anything? Are you hungry or thirsty?"

"I'm thirsty for you," I answered.

"Spartacus, you're sick."

"I'm sick from missing you."

"Oh, please."

"That's what you'll say when you beg me later," I replied before I coughed my lungs out.

"Wow, you're so seductive," she said and chuckled. "But I don't think anything is gonna happen today."

"In that case, you'll have to feed me."

She stood up and smiled. "That, I can do."

18

CHAPTER 18

TESLA

Spartacus was nowhere to be found when I opened my eyes. "Spartacus?" I called out, sitting in bed.

Maybe he went to the bathroom?

It was his third day of sick leave, and I was still his private Rewarder, but honestly, the man had been feigning his sickness since yesterday afternoon, and I just can't believe Gremelda fell for it—or even the doctor!

"Good morning," he said with a big smile as he came walking in the room with only a towel around his fucking hot waist. Ugh.

His skin still was a little damped and shiny and his dark hair dripped water onto his muscled chest. Why couldn't the man properly dry himself? And why was I always so damn horny in the morning? And why did I feel the urge to lick off those drizzling water beads that rolled over his hard little brown nipples? Fuck. I almost drooled on the sheets cause I forgot to swallow—something that normally never happens to me between the sheets.

"M-morning," I said, getting up and quickly heading to the bathroom to brush my teeth and take a shower. I mean, one can never know what would happen, right? I think it's only my duty as a Rewarder to always be clean and prepared for the Gladiator.

"I'll order us some breakfast!" I heard him shouting.

"Okay!" I replied before I closed the bathroom door.

Under the shower, I caught myself smiling when I thought I was yet to spend another day with him alone. Yesterday, we talked all day long. About our youth, the hotel, William, the Gladiator fights, his brother. I had said nothing about what happened before I got employed here. I didn't think Spartacus had anything to do with that or could do anything about it. He probably would only get worried.

He had been more open than I was, though. He'd shown me his brother and spoke about how hard things had been for him and his family. How hard they still were. His brother used to be a healthy young guy, but he couldn't do much after the accident anymore. But Spartacus really gained my respect for how he handled everything. He told me he started working here for his brother's health, too, saving for some operation that should make things a little better, though he would never be how he used to be.

I'd asked him why he suddenly told me all these private things since it had always been him who told me we couldn't tell each other about what our life was like before Invicta and that I couldn't call him by his name, yet now, he was suddenly more open.

The only thing he answered was that he trusted me for not telling anyone. I told him he could indeed trust me, cause I would not tell a soul.

I grabbed his shower gel and squeezed a big blob in my hand. I swear this stuff smelled the best, especially on him. I didn't care if it was a masculine scent. It smelled of caramel.

When I was ready, breakfast had already arrived, and we were now eating it on the couch.

"Why are you always so messy?" he asked, brushing my mouth at the corner with his thumb. "You're doing it on purpose, aren't you? Making me crazy..."

I scoffed. "I don't. And what? Crumbs make you go crazy?" I raised a brow.

"When you have them sticking to your lips, they do."

"Whatever pushes your buttons, I guess."

My personal buttons were mostly pushed by looking at his veiny forearms and the huge, hard, round pecs hidden underneath his tight white shirt. I came to know I loved him dressed in white.

He snatched the croissant from my hands. "You won't be needing this for now."

"Hey," I whined, but my breath immediately ran short when he pulled me to his lap. We were both wearing thin sweat shorts, and I could feel him harden underneath my weight. My body instantly followed his aroused state, and I felt myself getting wet. "I-I wasn't done with t-that yet," I stuttered breathlessly.

"Yes, you were," he replied. "When William wanted you, you refused him. You said you only had to sleep with a Gladiator if he wanted you to, as it's written in the contract. You only do what a Gladiator requests after he has won his match and picked you as a Rewarder."

"Uh, yeah," I answered.

"So... I have won no matches, you're not my Rewarder, and you can leave my room," he said, his large hands softly caressing my back and kneading my waist. "Or...you can stay, and we will break the rules together..."

Hm, I hadn't thought about it that way; I guess it would be like breaking the contract rules. Kinda.

"You know... some people say that rules are there to be broken, but I'm not one of them," I answered. He immediately looked like a sad puppy. "But maybe I will make an exception right now..."

I crashed my mouth against his and felt his hands sliding low. "Fuck," he hissed against my lips as he pushed them inside my pants and grabbed my booty.

While grinding crotch against his, I took off my shirt and then his, all while we never stopped kissing in between. I wasn't wearing a bra and pressed my breasts against his warm, hard chest, loving the way his enormous arms wrapped around my waist. God, I wanted to crawl under his skin so badly.

He gently pulled at my hair, making my head fall back before he kissed my neck, sucking at that one sensitive spot.

"Ahh..."

Heavy breaths filled the room as I let myself sink to the floor, where I took a position on my knees between his legs. I pulled his sweats off and teased him a little at first, kissing him from his knee to his navel and back to the other knee, obviously ignoring his massive hard-on. It took some willpower, though. I really wanted his taste on my tongue.

He looked at me with parted lips and horny eyes when I dropped my head between his legs and licked his balls first. As I massaged his perineum with my tongue, I grabbed his cock and started jerking him off at the same time.

"Shit, that feels good," he panted.

I kept doing what I did for a while until I took his cock in my mouth.

It didn't last long, though, before he said, "S-stop, or I'm gonna cum."

"Already?" I asked, rolling my tongue around the crown of the head.

"It's b-because you're so good at it," he replied, grabbing my arms and pulling me up to sit on his knee. "Couch or bed?" he asked.

"Bed."

He made me stand up straight and turned me around. His lips brushed against my ear while his hard cock pressed against my bum and his hands caressed front before he slowly pushed against me so that I walked to the bed, his mouth and hands never stopping what they did as he walked behind me.

"I love how you smell," he breathed against my ear.

"Thanks," I replied. "I l-love your scent too."

I felt heat rushing through my body, and I honestly don't think I've ever been this horny in my entire life. All I wanted was to feel him inside of me. Right now.

When my legs hit the bed, Spartacus turned me around and kissed me again before he kneeled to the floor and pulled my pants and panties down. He licked his way up, lips and stubbled chin brushing my legs but nowhere else, before he pushed me down to the mattress. I was fucking leaking like a broken faucet here.

He didn't join me in bed, though. He just stood there for a while, watching me in my shamefully aroused state.

Why was he taking his sweet time suddenly? Didn't he want me as much as I wanted him? "What's wrong?" I asked.

"Nothing's wrong. I'm just enjoying my view for a while."

"Well, come enjoy it here, in bed," I answered before I impatiently crawled further up the bed and spread myself for him, quite blatantly.

His smile disappeared like snow in the sun and made place for a look of hunger. He pinned himself on top of me. "You seem desperate for it, darling." He kissed my breasts, tongue bushing over my nipples, which he sucked hard, giving me all kinds of tingles.

Oh, I was desperate for it. "Fuck me," I ordered. He seemed to listen and positioned himself between my legs. But then he only caressed his cockhead against my entrance while kissing me again. I clenched against his cock. "Fuck me now," I breathed in his mouth.

While he smirked at me, I curled my legs around his hips, pulled him closer, and pushed my pussy to meet his cock, which slid inside of me. As it did, he grunted and kissed me hard before he pushed himself further inside until he was buried in me with all his many hard inches.

Fucking finally.

19

Chapter 19

Spartacus

"Jesus—wha—!" Gannicus cursed as I planted my fist into his stomach right before I finished him by giving a blow against his jaw. He flew a meter further and landed on his back where he started to laugh as he spat out some blood. "What... the... fuck... man?" he asked, breathless. "You were... just sick! You shouldn't be—" I pulled him up from the ground. "T-this... strong...."

Well, what could I say? I felt great. I felt better than I had felt in years. Things finally seemed to all fall into place for good ol' Dean. I made good money, I worked with lovely friends and now I have also gotten myself the girl that I've been longing and pining for for all these years. She wasn't my girlfriend yet, but I was gonna make her mine. Soon.

"I agree, it's not fair. When I recovered from flu not too long ago, I was a fucking wreck for weeks! And you just waltz back into training and resume to be the best of us all," Crixus shook his head. "Ugh. Not fair, I tell ya. Not fair."

I grinned like an idiot, thinking back about my "sick leave". I had only been sick for half of it. The other half of the time, I was fucking Ryah to heaven and back.

"Oh, fuck—oh, fuck me! I'm so close, S-spartacus," she moaned.

"Dean," I corrected her before I grabbed her hips tighter and slammed myself into her, deeper than before.

It started to irritate me when she moaned out the name Spartacus. I know it was I that ordered her to call me by that name but there was this urge inside of me to hear her moan out my real name. It had been on my mind for quite some time now.

"Hahhh—D-dean, ahh...!" she cried out.

It had been so fucking beautiful to hear it spilling from her lips. Dean.

"I need to let these war wounds be treated," Gannicus announced, snapping me out of my thoughts, and he left me and Crixus to go and get himself some assistance with his injuries.

"You wanna train with the net?" I asked Crixus as I wiped off some sand from my arms. I really wondered why Gremelda didn't just give us an arena with a mat or something. But no, she wanted to keep the sand because it was just like the good old days.

"No fucking way," he replied. "Wanna do swords?"

"Neh, just did that before my fight with Gannicus. Lasso?"

"My God, you know I hate that even more than the net," Crixus answered. "I'm just gonna practice on spear throwing."

"Ok, dude," I answered.

Maybe I could practice my blind fighting skills with Oenomaus or something. I really needed to do that, even though I didn't want to. However, right now, I was in a good mood, and I felt that nothing could get me in a grumpy mood.

"I can't handle that disgusting happy grin on your face anyway," Crixus said, making me laugh. "I don't like you like this. Your face looks so happy, it's scary."

"How's your dick, by the way?" I asked him. "Is it still attached to your body?"

"Shut up." He laughed too. "At least be careful, man, because I know why you're smiling, and I don't want you to get into trouble or whatever."

In the evening, I had snuck into Ryah's room, where we currently laid in her bed, watching some show. I wasn't paying attention to the tv, though, as all my attention went to her. The way she felt in my arms, so soft and smooth and squeezable. The way she smelled, the way her body rocked up and down as she breathed slowly. She was warm and she made me feel warm too.

When the show was over, she rolled off my chest and onto her belly, looking at me. "Do you ever miss the people back home, your friends and family, I mean? I'm missing my parents more these last few weeks." She sighed.

"I do," I admitted. "Why do you suddenly miss them more?"

"I don't know."

"Are you unhappy in Invicta?"

"No, not at all," she replied.

"That's cool. I would be kinda offended if you had said that you were," I replied, smiling.

"I'm not. I don't think I ever said it before, but Bentley is actually my best friend. We've known each other for a few years already."

"Yeah, I kinda figured that out that day you came back drunk from the boss's office. You called her Shana instead of Bentley. I could feel that you girls had a bond."

"Gosh, don't remind me of that night."

I pinched her nose. "You were cute."

She slapped my hand away but smiled at me. "I was shameless." She then shamefully laid her forehead against my chest.

"Speaking of our boss, why is that man still here?" I asked. "I would have thought he would leave straight away but he's been here for a few days already."

Ryah looked up at me and bit her lip before she laid her head on my chest again, this time taking a comfortable position, and said, "I don't know...."

"Are you sure?" I asked. The way she said it made me a little suspicious. "You don't have to answer me. You can also say that you don't want to answer, then I'll leave it, but I don't want you to lie to me."

It was quiet in the room for some time.

"I guess it's maybe because of me. But I'm not sure."

I wiggled myself out of her embrace and sat up. I guess she just gave me the green light to keep on asking. "What do you mean?"

"Well, before I got a job here, something happened...." She sat up too. "I sometimes got hired for stuff and this time I got paid to go on a date—"

"You mean you worked as a—"

"No! Not as an escort or anything, if that's what you mean. I was only paid to go on a date, nothing more," she clarified. "Anyway, in the middle of the date, the guy told me I needed to leave. I found it strange because I thought we had good fun and I kinda liked him.

Ok, that made me jealous, but I swallowed it away as she continued the story.

"And then... that guy got murdered after I left the date. And on top of that, he appeared to be a shady kinda cop, a dirty cop. His family is known in the underworld. In fact, he was a cousin of William."

"No way... Did you know William too?" I asked.

"No, I just found out that they were cousins the day I was ordered by William to follow him. He then told me. I'd never seen him before."

Murder, dirty cops, underworld. This sounded like bad news to me. I didn't like this at all! "They all think that you killed that guy?" I asked.

"No, nobody thinks I did it... or maybe the cops do, I don't even know. Pfff, it's all just such a mess!" She sighed. "But at least William seems to believe me, and he said that he will deal with it all. That I can leave Invicta when it's all cleared."

"And you trust his words?" I asked.

"Yeah, I do." There was no hesitation in her voice whatsoever.

I really hoped she was right. What if something happened to her? "I don't like this."

"Hey... it's gonna be ok. See? That's why I didn't tell you. You're the kind of man that gets worried straight away."

"Well, can you blame me?" I asked.

She crawled closer and kissed me on the lips. "You don't seem worried that we are doing this behind Invicta's back...."

She had a point there. "Actually, until William has sorted it out, maybe we shouldn't," I replied.

"Are you kidding me?" She pushed me on my back and straddled me. "You shouldn't always change your mind about things. Don't do that. Besides that, I'm a grown woman too, even older than you are, and I'm saying we won't stop this."

Pathetic as I was, when her lips and tongue hit my neck, I was already mush. "And who says that you are the boss?"

"Well, you're not my Gladiator now, you didn't win me, so... right now, I'm promoting myself to being your boss."

CHAPTER 20

TESLA

I got news that every employee of the Gladiator/Rewarder team was going to receive a small bonus because the hotel had made some good money this quarter due to the bets that were made. Madame Gremelda had just informed me and after she did, she ordered me to send Mercedes to her office.

I was too happy with the bonus to have my mood ruined completely but I had to say that Mercedes kinda scared me. She always looked at me with eyes that wanted me to drop dead or something.

"Uh, Mercedes?" I asked after I entered the gym and approached her. She always hung out here every day, working on her physique while I was just a lazyass and only worked out twice or thrice a week. I had the advantage that I was naturally curvy in all the right places and could eat whatever I wanted without paying attention to the scale.

"What?" she asked, not looking at me while running breathlessly on the treadmill.

"Gremelda needs you right now."

"Right now?"

"Yeah, her specific words were 'send Mercedes to my office next', so..." I shrugged. I was just here to deliver the message.

"Ugh, fine." She stopped the treadmill, stepped off, and stood before me with a displeased look in her eyes. "Can you move out of the way? I need my towel."

"Oh, yeah. Sorry." I took a step to the side so she could reach for the towel. When she turned around, she bumped against my shoulder which was unnecessary in my eyes as she had enough space to move. "Do you have a problem with me, Cedi?" I asked.

"It's Mercedes for you, not Cedi, I'm not your friend," she answered as she dried her sweaty face and left without saying another word. My question stayed unanswered, although I kind of knew the answer to it already.

Jeez. What a bitch!

"Yo, Tesla!" Mahindra called out from the other side of the gym.

This sports center was so big and luxurious and was only for us. It was ridiculous if you asked me. There were at most like five Rewarders a day training here since the Gladiators had their own gym. It was bonkers.

Right now, only Mahindra and buff guy were here. I learned his name was Mustang. He was cool. Nice guy.

As I walked towards Mahindra, I greeted Mustang, but he was too busy to hear me, pressing God only knows how many kilos as he laid down on the bench. I wondered if those veins popping on his forehead were healthy because it looked quite concerning to me.

"Hey, Mahindra," I said and dropped down on one of the seats of the fitness equipment next to him.

He placed the set of dumbells back again and wiped his face dry.

"Hey. So, I heard we're getting bonuses?"

"I'm not sure. I only know that I got one," I answered.

He sighed. "I haven't been picked all that often this month. So, maybe nothing for me...."

"You're just gonna have to wait," I replied, not really knowing what to say otherwise.

"It could also be that a big guest is coming," he said.

"Oh? Why do you think that?"

"Gremelda usually throws out bonuses if something is up. I dunno, I can't prove it, but it's something I have noticed. And it often is when an important guest will come."

"Aha."

He took a gulp from his water bottle and stood up, walking to the next machine. "So, we haven't talked all too much since you're working here since it was Bentley that took you under her wing, but how are you? Do you like it here?" he asked.

"I'm pretty pleased with life right now," I replied, honestly.

I was pretty pleased indeed. Especially when I laid in bed with a certain Gladiator.... That man could please the shit out of me.

"Well, you certainly had a good start." He smiled. "I mean you're the new star Rewarder and you've been that since your very first day."

"I'm not complaining."

We chatted some more while he continued to work on his body and I continued to be my lazy self before he stood up and said he would shower.

"Okay, I'll go to my room, man," I said. "See you."

"Yeah, see you later. Bye, ma'am."

That afternoon, I spent time with Bentley at the pool on the roof, getting a bit of a tan. The weather was great.

Too bad that Spartacus had to practice almost every day. It would be nice to hang out with him here, laying together at the pool, enjoying the sun. Although, maybe we shouldn't. It would be hard to keep my eyes and hands off of him if I saw him wearing only swim shorts. We couldn't let anybody find out that we had this little understanding about seeing each other between work.

I should just be a little bit more patient. He was going to come to my room tonight and the thought alone made me feel all tingly inside. I wondered what we were to each other if I had to give it a name. Maybe we were dating? It wasn't just fucking that we did. We talked, we cuddled, we laughed. Though it was a lot of fucking too of course... which I didn't mind at all! We had been doing this for a few weeks already and every day I was waiting to see him, more eager than the day before.

"Fuck, I'm tired," Bentley said.

"Didn't you sleep well?"

"Nah, I watched porn till three," she answered, yawning. "I'm happy that there is a match tomorrow. I hope I'll get picked, cause I need myself some cock asap."

Poor girl. "I don't really know what to say to that."

"You're getting cock regularly so you don't understand my pain."

"True."

"The last few times, I got picked by that new Gladiator, Verus, and he only wants to talk and have his cock sucked off. I don't even get any," she whispered so nobody would hear her. "You know how fucking frustrating that is? Why doesn't Gannicus just pick me, pffff."

I patted her shoulder. "Sorry, girl."

She finished her drink and laid down again. "Okay, I'm gonna sleep a little. Wake me up in a few hours."

"I will."

As she slept, I daydreamed. I relaxed in the sun and in my mind were muscular thighs, solid abs, and a hard long cock, pounding inside of me.

There were worse ways to spend your afternoon, I supposed.

"Hey, darling," Spartacus said after he entered my room and I closed the door.

I grabbed him by his shoulders and pushed him against the door before I kissed him on the lips.

"Hi, sir..." I answered after I withdrew my tongue out of his mouth.

He was breathless. "Jesus... that's another way of saying h-hi. Have you missed me?"

I smirked at him and brushed the tip of my nose against his nose. He then grabbed my ass and turned us around so it was me that was pressed against the door. He pushed his hips against mine and I felt a spark of electricity running up my spine, making me even more desperate than I already was.

Holy fucking shit, this man turned me on so, so much.

We kissed our way to the couch where he sat down and I crawled on his lap.

Right when I wanted to rip off his shirt, a familiar beep was heard. My front door flew open and my best friend rushed inside. Bentley looked afraid, sad, and shocked, but it wasn't surprise in her eyes at seeing me sitting on Spartacus on a night that we weren't supposed to be sitting like this. It was something else.

"What's wrong?" I asked, crawling off the Gladiator's lap.

"Mahindra! Someone killed him!" Bentley cried out.

"What?!" Spartacus asked and stood up. I did the same. "What happened?"

"They say he had a bag over his head. He's dead! Oh my God, that poor guy! He's dead!" My friend kept repeating.

How could this be? I didn't understand. Violence was something that never happened here. That's what they said—violence isn't allowed. "But how—"

"Invicta's police are everywhere in the building. It's fucking scary!" Bentley added.

"Jesus." I felt my heart skip a beat. "I just talked to him today," I whispered and sat back down.

It felt so strange. How was this possible?

21

Chapter 21

SPARTACUS

About one minute after Bentley had entered the room, all our phones started to buzz. There was a message from Gremelda. It said that we were to gather in the meeting room in ten minutes, lined up. There was important news.

Never has something like this occurred in all the time I worked here. Sure, there were some quarrels between guests, but it was always solved quickly. They weren't stupid, they knew better than to anger Hotel Invicta. And now someone was very possibly killed, and it wasn't even one of the guests but a member of the hotel staff.

Tesla, Bentley, and I walked in silence, all of us still shocked by the news. As soon as we entered the meeting room, we took our positions. I hated that I couldn't stand close to Tesla.

When I looked at Cedi, I felt so sorry for the girl. She had puffy eyes and a red nose. I knew Mahindra was her friend here so this must come as an even greater shock to her. The other Rewarders looked shocked as well and some Gladiators had shimmering eyes too, especially the ones that had spent more time with the guy. I didn't know him all that well.

I just realized that we were never going to find out who the real Mahindra actually was. What was his name? And what will Invicta even do with him? They couldn't tell his parents or other family members what he was doing here.

Gremelda walked in, guarded by what seemed to be at least two dozen of armed guards. William, however, was absent. I expected him to be with her since the guy has never left the hotel, but I guess he must be dealing with Invicta's police himself.

Gremelda let out a deep sigh before she started to talk.

"I zink most of you have already heard vat is going on in zee hotel. But for zee ones zat haven't heard: Mahindra is dead," she spoke calmly. Cedi and the Asian twins let out a loud sob.

I saw Gremelda swallow. She would never let it out herself, would never cry in front of us, but I knew her well enough to see she was struggling with this. Mahindra was a Rewarder and I knew how Gremelda felt about us underneath that hard appearance. She was a mother hen, and the Rewarders and the Gladiators were her babies. And she must be angry. Very angry.

We all kept quiet, letting her talk. She informed us that Invicta was dealing with the situation but all matches were canceled until the killer was found. That meant that all activities involving both Gladiators and Rewarders were paused.

"Zer is ein reason we have decided to take zis drastic decision," she continued. "Reason for it is zat we believe zat Mahindra's death was ein warning for another one of zee Rewarders."

Did I hear that correctly? I heard some gasps around me, so I guess I did. I instantly looked at Tesla and she instantly looked at me. I tried to stay focused to hear what Gremelda was saying next.

She told us that we would have to stay in our rooms in pairs: One Gladiator and One Rewarder would stay together. The rooms were going to be guarded by two armed guards. We would not be permitted to leave, only when we had to talk to the head of Invicta's special team for research purposes.

One by one she called names. Tesla and I were announced to share a room, and selfish as I was in a time like this, the idea of spending so much time with her alone felt amazing.

We were guarded by the promised two guards to my room and they locked us in while they stood outside.

"This feels so surreal," Tesla said as she walked to the refrigerator. She let out a disappointed sigh when she couldn't find anything that contained alcohol. "I'm calling room service. You think I can do that now?"

"I guess yeah, why not?"

"I don't know, cause they don't think me drinking alcohol is important at the moment... but, ugh, fuck it. I need to get hammered."

"No, you don't," I replied.

"Yes, I do," she said, a little annoyed. "That's how I deal with issues. I get hammered, ok?"

She ordered some stuff and I just let her. We went to sit on the couch, where we sat for a while in silence again, both processing the new information.

I looked to my side and found her biting her nails. I gently pulled her fingers out of her mouth and grabbed her head, turning it to face me. "Don't do that," I softly said, releasing her face again. "You don't think this has anything to do with you, do you?" I then asked. Please let her say no.

"The thought has crossed my mind." She bit her lower lip.

That wasn't what I wanted to hear. Fuck.

"Why?" I asked.

"I don't know. But..." She sighed. "First, a man died shortly after he told me to leave a date, which was all very weird to begin with. And now someone else was killed that was very possibly a warning for another Rewarder. I-I don't know, I just have this weird feeling inside my gut, you know? This can't be all just a coincidence." Her voice was shaky. "I'm also starting to believe that William has arranged for me to come to this hotel in the first place. Bentley told me that Gremelda asked if she knew someone, and here's the weird part: only Bentley was asked, not any of the other Rewarders."

Ok, I had to agree that it did sound a little suspicious.

"He did it to protect you?" I asked. I mean, I thought William was an arrogant douche (even though I would never say that out loud) but maybe something bad would have happened to Ryah already if she was out there. I think if William really had planned this, he would have never thought someone had the balls or the knowledge to enter this place. He must be fucking fuming.

"I don't know," she said again, shaking her head. "I think I just have to wait until I can speak to the investigating team or something—or to William."

I nodded. "At least you're safe here. I will never leave your side and outside are two huge bears carrying machine guns." I wrapped my arm around her. "I'll never let you get harmed, ok? I'm no small man and am a professional fighter. I'll rip the guy's head off." I swear I would. "But you gotta tell me everything from now on."

She nodded and turned her head to me, letting out a small smile before she looked all serious again. "I just really hope it has nothing to do with me, because—because if it does, then it means that M-Mahindra is dead because of me."

"Hey, it's not because of you, ok?" I replied. "It's because there is some crazy lunatic out there who did this horrible thing."

"..."

"You know what? Shall I run us a bath?" I asked.

"Yeah... I'd like that."

During the time the bath was getting ready, room service had brought Tesla her booze. We now laid in the bathtub. She was settled between my legs, her back to my chest, while she was occasionally sipping on some wine.

I gently caressed her arms.

"I'm not gonna get hammered," she said, breaking the silence. "I choose this way of dealing with shit over getting drunk."

22

Chapter 22

BENTLEY

I could just smell trouble coming. And right now, this foul odor told me that Mahindra's death probably had something to do with Ryah in some way, and that concerned me to no end.

Ryah had said that she told me all there was to tell, and I believed her, but this all couldn't be a coincidence either, right? No. I dared to say it wasn't, and little old me was always right. (At least ninety-nine percent of the time.)

I was heartbroken about Mahindra's death. We all had a lot to process today. But right now, my mind was with Ryah, praying she would stay safe. I hated I couldn't be around her, but I trusted Spartacus and I really believed he liked Ryah. Plus, he was the number one fighter, so I knew my friend was safe with him, which gave me a little peace.

And here I was... stuck with the only Gladiator that had a huge mommy complex.

We sat on the couch, Gannicus on the left and I on the right.

"Gremelda must be so worried," he said once more. I think this was the fourth time he talked about Gremelda's worries and it honestly started to piss me off.

"I swear to God if you say that one more time, I'll bite your throat off," I replied.

"Jesus, Bent." He softly punched against my shoulder. "I know it must freak you out they said the killer is after one of the Rewarders, but let's stay nice to each other, please. Or are you jealous? Because you think I like Gremelda more than I like you?"

Gannicus had often picked me, and we talked for nights, so I knew all about him. His childhood had been hard. His mother died of cancer after battling the horrible disease for years and he slowly saw her slipping away from his hands. His last partner was his substitute mommy, and she dumped him before he came to Invicta.

Gannicus never really cared about the "let's not talk about our past" rule.

I was pretty positive he only thought he liked Gremelda, but he didn't, really. I mean, what's there to like? The woman was a bitch. Plus, she would never fall for someone like Gannicus.

Right now, I didn't even know if I liked the man or hated his guts. I felt I needed to scold him right now.

"Someone died, you twat! And someone else could be in danger. So no, I'm not jealous of Gremelda. I'm stressed. And I don't care about her worries, I care about mine."

"Okay... okay..." He held his hands in the air, apologizing, "I'm sorry."

I sighed. "It's fine. I guess this day has been weird for all of us."

"It has. My God, who would have guessed this? But luckily, you're here with me. I'll keep you safe, babe," he promised with his hand on his heart.

At the moment, I needed something more than his arms around me to keep me safe. I needed his dick to destress from all this shit. With hungry eyes, I found myself staring at his crotch, my eyes following the contours of this bulge. This lack of sex was really getting to me.

The thing with Gannicus was that he was a hunter. If I was going to be all desperate for it, he wouldn't want me. I realized that the last couple of times, when it had been me that was lusting for him but became his psychiatrist instead of his filthy whore.

And, shit, how I wanted to be his filthy whore so badly! Luckily, I had my ways, and I usually got what I wanted. (At least ninety-nine percent of the time.)

"Don't think that you can lay a finger on me, you got that? Not one," I cried out. "No touching. We're not at work here."

"I know it's against the rules, babe. Of course, there will be no touching, fumbling, or fucking. I wasn't even talking about that. I simply said I'll keep you safe... But..." He caressed my cheek. "Don't make me laugh. I know you want this dick." He grabbed my hand and laid it on his crotch.

I almost wanted to beg him to take me, but I stayed strong and pulled my hand back. "Ew. No thanks."

I just showered and was clean as a whistle, wearing only a little white towel around my body.

Smirking to myself in the mirror, I ran a hand through my wet hair, pushing the black long locks to the back. "Oops, I forgot to take underwear with me. What must I do now?" I whispered to my reflection.

I quickly brushed my teeth so that my breath was all fresh and minty before I winked at the mirror. "Come on, Shana. You're sexy, you're hot, and you still got this," I gave myself some courage before heading out the door.

Back in the living room, I sashayed my hips in the most sensual way possible and noticed I soon had Gannicus's attention.

"Forgot my underwear," I said, heading towards the bedroom. "Oh, wait." I slapped against my forehead. "I haven't unpacked yet. Duh."

I walked to the suitcase, ducked down to open it, pointing my ass at the Gladiator. If I had aimed right, he had an unobstructed view of a very special smooth hairless pink flower right now.

"Uh-Bentley..."

"Hm?" I hummed in question, pretending I couldn't find my underwear, ignoring the dozen lace panties that already went through my hands while I really bent and ducked to search in this suitcase, oh my.

After what felt like forever, he answered. "I can see, uh—" He cleared his throat.

"What can you see, Gannicus?" I asked before I stood up, turned around, and faced him. I actually counted on him standing up to assault me from behind, but sadly, my plan had failed. Damn it! Time for Plan B! I accidentally unfolded my towel, which fell to the ground.

"...!"

"Whoopsie," I said. After I picked the towel up, I wrapped it around my body again, this time a little higher. Maybe he hadn't seen the candy at my last attempt. To make sure he would this time, I turned around and ducked down, slightly spreading my legs before I searched for my underwear one more time. feeling the cool air of the AC hitting my pussy and crack.

"You're so obvious," he said in a hoarse voice.

I finally grabbed a red lingerie set and put it on. "I don't know what you mean? Besides that, it's not like you've never seen this before."

I let my hands caress me from collar bones to hips, stroking over the red lace.

"You're clearly trying to horn me up."

"What makes you think so?" I asked.

"Okay, you win. Damn it, come here, you little minx!"

"No. No fucking." I shook my finger in the air.

"Oh, come on!" he whined.

"No fucking," I said again, pressing my hand into my panties to stroke my pussy. I always loved to tease desperate men.

"Well, what should I do now, then? I'm hard as steel here!" he said with frustration. "You purposely showed me that pussy and ass and you know it!"

I was having trouble holding my laugh.

"I was searching for my underwear, Gannicus."

"Fuck you, woman, and come here."

I couldn't help but smirk while I rushed over to him and straddled his lap, grinding my private parts against his abs in the process. His muscles weren't so huge as some other Gladiators' were, but they were so hard you could grate cheese on them. Fucking hot!

He kissed me with passion and moaned into my mouth how I was the hottest one of all and why it had been so long since we fucked. Ugh, what an idiot.

Anyway, I got my way, and I guessed Madame Gremelda was all forgotten now!

23

Chapter 23

TESLA

"Sit down, Tesla," William ordered, gesturing his hand to an empty chair.

I sat down opposite of him, the desk in the middle of us. Behind William stood two other men who looked like you didn't want to mess with them, dressed in all black and broad as bears.

Madame Gremelda was there too, pouring water into a glass. It was for me.

"Thank you."

"You're welcome," she replied, taking her place on the other empty chair next to William.

The boss then laid something flat on the table and shoved it towards me. I waited until he told me I should take a look. When I did, I saw it was a Polaroid picture.

The image in the photo left me in shock.

It was Mahindra's face, his dead face. But he was shown in the background, a little blurry. There was a hand in the foreground, the index and middle fingers making a V shape, gesturing a peace sign. On the index finger, a small black triangle tattoo decorated the olive-toned skin.

I knew that tattoo. "No," I whispered, inhaling deeply while I felt my throat getting tighter and tighter. "No, no, no."

"You recognise the tattoo, don't you?" William asked calmly.

"...!" It felt as if I couldn't breathe anymore. My heart pounded against my ribs while a wave of fear and panic rushed through my body. Yes, I recognised that tattoo. It belonged to one of my exes, Reggie.

What I feared was true. Mahindra was dead because of me!

"Hey, easy there," William said, and he stood up, walked around the desk and kneeled beside me.

"I can't—cannot b-breathe," I said, choking on my own spit. Sweat started to pour from every pore I had on my body, and I felt like I was dying. Maybe I was dying. Maybe Reggie had already broken into the hotel and drugged me. Oh my God, I was going to die!

"You're having a panic attack, Tesla," William said before he sent the others out of the room for a moment. "You have had this before; you can get out of it. Breathe."

How the fuck did he know?

I shook my head. "N-no, I—I'm dying."

Out of panic, I grabbed his shoulders and breathed against his face.

Help me.

"You will not die. Breathe," he said again before he started breathing together with me like I was having a fucking baby and he was the father. "Do you want me to leave too?"

"No, don't leave."

I shook my head and tried to breathe in as deeply as I could. I closed my eyes and tried to think about other stuff to focus on. But how the fuck could I think about something else when someone died because of me. He was dead! Because of me!

OH GOD.

Twenty minutes later, William had somehow gotten me to calm down. I didn't die, but I felt like shit.

The others were back, too. Gremelda looked at me with sympathy, a look I had never seen on her before.

"As soon as they delivered the picture this morning, I knew you were the Rewarder that is in danger," William said. "Of course, I suspected that already, but now I was sure."

"You probably know all about Reggie then?" I asked, my voice still shaking.

William nodded. "I suspected it ever since Ramone died," William explained.

"You're the one who lured me into working here, aren't you?"

"I was. This hotel is the safest place you can be…" William sighed through his nose. "Though… I hate to say that after what just happened. This was never supposed to happen, so you can imagine I am very, very angry. And my pride has taken a colossal blow. However, an employee died and another is in danger, so I suppose I have to shove my pride to the side and deal with this as a grown-up."

I had so many fucking questions right now, but I stayed silent until William was done talking.

"But that fucker," he continued, "is smart."

I knew Reggie was a smart man, having an IQ above 160. He was also crazy.

Very crazy.

Maybe even a stone-cold psychopath.

He and I were actually pretty happily in love for a few weeks, but then he started acting crazy and obsessed with all sorts of things, so I dumped his ass. I've had him stalking me for a while after we split up, but he stopped that a year ago and it was never anything serious or dangerous. I can't believe he snapped like this. Truthfully, I was scared shitless of him now.

"He is," I agreed.

"Do you know how painful it is for a man like myself to deal with a man that outsmarts me and my entire team? It hurts, Tesla. It fucking hurts. At this moment, I am so frustrated, I would give my left ball to catch him and break his neck. I'm not even lying here."

"Ow-kay..." I looked at Madame Gremelda and she nodded at me, silently agreeing that William was indeed very angry.

This situation looked like a fucking movie. It was as if I had stepped into some bad mystery thriller. But one thing didn't click with me. Why was Reggie after Ramone? I asked William about it because it made little sense to me.

"Ah, I'm afraid, that's just bad luck on my cousin's side. I can never be sure, since I can't ask someone who is buried six feet under, but I think Ramone saw Reggie when you were at the restaurant, and he probably thought the guy was there for him. The restaurant owner saw Ramone threatening him, and later, my cousin laid dead in the toilet."

"So... Ramone is also dead because of me?" Panic rose to my head again.

"No. Ramone is dead because of that psychopath. What happened between you and him?"

"Reggie is... insane, but he can act like he is not. He can be charming and caring; basically, he can pretend to be someone else.

But he can't keep up with that, because eventually he'll start to show little fragments of his true nature. And I never believed it when people warned me about him. I believed his act. But later, I found out." I took a sip of water. My mouth was so dry. "He-he got jealous. Like, really annoyingly jealous. Then he turned manipulative. He started lying. Actually, he probably always lied, but now I'd find out. He wanted things his way or not at all. I just couldn't stand him anymore when his actual personality presented itself from behind the mask. So I broke up with him."

"Then?" William asked.

"Everything was ok at first. He cried, but he said he understood. A little later, he sometimes sat in my house when I returned from work. I—I got scared then. I filed for a restraining order but failed. However, he was suddenly gone. I haven't seen him since."

I bit the hard skin around my left thumbnail till it hurt.

"Listen." William bent over the desk and grabbed my hand in his, plucking it out of my mouth. "I was arrogant, thinking nobody would get into this place and start drama. Now, I've learned from my mistakes, and I promise you that nobody will enter the floor where you're staying. I even have someone guarding the fucking vent pipe exits to be sure."

I bit my lip and nodded. "Thanks."

"Don't worry, Tesla. Invicta will get him. Zis will all be over soon," Gremelda said, approaching me. She laid her hand on my shoulder and rubbed it awkwardly.

Their words were comforting, but I was scared anyway.

At night, I laid in Dean's arms. I'd just stopped crying again. That two people had died because of my crazy ex and this hotel had to invest so much in stopping him made me feel so bad.

"Are you okay like this?" he asked.

I nodded against his chest. "Yeah."

"Can I do anything for you?"

"No, you've already done everything I can ask for."

He was so sweet, hearing me out, comforting me, and talking to me. He looked under the bed and in every closet and space that someone might use to hide. He even put a glass of water on the bedside table because he noticed I often got out of bed during the night to drink some water in the kitchen. He also said I should wake him up if I needed to pee at night.

Reggie was a head shorter than Spartacus was, and quite a scrawny guy. But it wasn't his body size I was afraid of. It was his mind. His capability of thinking something we didn't catch. I saw danger in everything and everywhere now. And I was also scared for Spartacus's safety. What if Reggie knew about him and was jealous?

Fuck, I needed to stop these thoughts for now. I didn't want to worry Spartacus more than he already was. I just wanted to fall asleep like this and wake up with the news that William caught that bastard.

Chapter 24

SPARTACUS

I looked at my brother lying in bed, who'd just turned his head from left to right. He was still okay. My heart was eased once more when I disconnected the connection and my screen turned black.

When William told me he had arranged for some guards to watch our families as well (just to be sure of their safety), I'd become so worried for my brother that I now checked him at least once every hour. Each time I saw him moving, making one of those slight motions he still was able to make, was a blessing for my eyes.

I changed my mind about the boss. He seemed to be an okay guy for doing all of this. He was also going all out to help Ryah in this whole drama. Maybe it was because he had kind of failed to provide enough safety in the hotel in the first place, but still.

Ryah told me her ex was insane, and I had no doubts about that. The guy had to be insane, daring to outnumber an underworld boss like this. I'm sure William had a complete team of experts behind him. Yet, they still hadn't caught the guy.

So now, Ryah was a mess. She cried often, feeling guilty about everything. It wasn't her fault, though. Every day, I told her she wasn't responsible for the actions of other people, but I also knew this was easier said than done. If I were her, I would also feel terrible.

Having that strange feeling of being watched, I looked up and found Ryah looking at me while she stood in the kitchen and I sat on the couch.

"What's wrong?" I asked.

"Nothing. I was just thinking how great you are."

I stood up and walked over to her. Standing behind her back, wrapping my arms around her as she was busy grabbing a bag of chips from one of the high-hanging cabinets, I said, "I think you're pretty great yourself."

She hummed, put the bag of chips down on the countertop, and rubbed one of her hands over my thigh.

I kissed her neck, testing if I was allowed. Did she want me to touch her? Did she need this or not? When no protest came, I started to suck on her skin some more, drawing my lips to the other side of her neck, tasting the little bit of saltiness of fresh sweat.

She turned around and slammed her lips against mine. I guess she wanted me, so I hoisted her up and planted her ass on top of the kitchen counter, spreading her legs so I could stand between them. Her arms and legs wrapped around my waist as she hungrily devoured my lips, taking off her shirt in the process. It was clear she was in need of some control after all that had happened, so I let her. I wished I could make things better for her, wished I could take all this drama away. Unfortunately, I couldn't. I could only be there for her. "You are so beautiful," I panted into her mouth. "And sweet and smart and funny."

"So many compliments," she replied, smiling against my lips. "Let's go to the bedroom and fuck me there, will you?"

"I just wanted to let you know."

"You're sweet." She chuckled. "Now fuck me."

I lifted her and carried her to the bed, where I gently laid her down and kissed her some more before we both undressed until we were nude.

"Dean?"

"Hm?" I asked, hovering over her. God, I loved the touch of her naked body against mine.

"If we ever get out of here, ask me out on a date again."

I smiled at her. "Are you trying to say something here, darling?"

"Yeah. I'm trying to say... I really like you, so if you would ever want to ask me out again, I'll say yes."

"I really like you too," I answered, my mouth curling into a gigantic smile.

The first time we did it, I didn't fuck her at all. Instead, she rode me so slow, intense, and pleasurable, I almost lost all my marbles.

"So, he drives you mad?" Ryah asked, speaking through the phone.

Madame Gremelda had allowed her and Bentley to call each other once a day. I guess Gremelda pitied her.

"Haha. Jesus, woman, why do you always have to be so vulgar?" she asked, shaking her head while she smiled.

Well, in that case, Bentley suited Gannicus just perfectly, because that man's other name was vulgar.

"Well, attend to his and your needs, then. I know I just did...." She then looked at me with a smirk on her face. I'm glad she seemed a little happier again.

A knock against the door pricked my ears, followed by William's voice, telling us it was him and he would come inside.

"Gotta go, the boss is here." Ryah hung up just as William opened the door and walked in, accompanied by two guards.

"How's life over here?" the boss asked, scanning the room. I hoped there weren't things lying around that could give away what we just did.

Three times...

"Is there any news?" Ryah asked, ignoring his question.

"No, I'm afraid not." William sat on the couch. Right where we had enjoyed the second round of sweet, sweet pleasure.

I cleared my throat thinking back about it.

"So, Tesla, I've talked to Gremelda, and she said you're crying a lot." William patted the empty cushion next to him for Ryah to sit down. Somehow, that irked me a bit. The woman wasn't a dog.

"Well, a lot, a lot..." Ryah softly replied. "I wouldn't really call it a lot under these circumstances."

"How about panic attacks? Have you experienced more of those after the one in my office?"

"..."

"Did she?" William asked, looking at me.

"Yeah, she did," I answered, making Ryah peek at me. She didn't look angry, though, so I hoped it was okay.

"I think it's best if I send Dr. Rosenfeld to you. He's our hotel psychiatrist," William suggested. "You can trust him."

"Hotel psychiatrist?" Ryah asked.

"Yes. It would surprise you to know how often guests need him. There is nothing to be ashamed about. He's there to listen to you."

Ryah plucked at her nails again. If I thought they were a mess before, I could think again. "I can talk to Spartacus."

William slapped her plucking hand away from the wounded one. Again, I was irritated, but I also found myself ridiculous to get jealous at a time like this. I just wanted to sit next to her and hold her hand, but I couldn't, or William would know all about our secret relationship.

"Spartacus isn't a trained professional. There's been a lot going on in your life that is hard to process, so, I'm sending Dr. Rosenfeld. End of discussion."

CHAPTER 25

TESLA

"Good afternoon," a rather short, middle-aged man said as he walked into the room, followed by the boss. He stuck out his hand, which was encased in rubber. "I'm Dr. Rosenfeld." His blue eyes looked at me from behind thick black glasses.

"I'm Tesla," I answered, grabbing his hand.

William closed the door. "Doc has a bit of a phobia for germs, hence the gloves."

"A-hah," I answered.

"Psychiatrists are also only human after all," the bearded psychiatrist said with a smile.

I gave him a quick smile back before I looked at William. "I still don't think all this is necessary."

"Tesla, we've had this conversation already," William responded, a bit annoyed.

I rubbed my sweaty palms against my sweatpants and walked further into the room, dropping to the couch.

Spartacus introduced himself to Dr. Rosenfeld as well before the man covered the sitting cushion of one of the large armchairs opposite me with a crisp white handkerchief and sat down on it. "We will not do anything you don't like. We'll just talk. Is that okay with you?"

Knowing I had no other choice, I nodded in agreement. "Okay."

"I usually have the sessions with my clients alone, but if you want, we can let William stay with us," the doctor offered.

I didn't want William to stay. I wanted Spartacus to stay. But I couldn't say that. I also didn't want William to think of me as some loser he had to hold hands with, so I answered it was fine by me if William left.

"Call me when you're done," William told Dr. Rosenfeld as he stood up. He ordered Spartacus to follow him, granting us some privacy.

Spartacus followed him but looked at me once before he left the room, giving me a little wink. I instantly felt better. He made me feel all warm and fuzzy inside.

"Uh—do you want something to drink?" I asked after the others were gone, lusting for a cold beer myself.

"No, thank you. I drink nothing that I haven't bought or brought and have disinfected myself. Plus, I just had a large cup of coffee."

"Must be hard to have such a condition," I said.

"It's not ideal, but I have been able to live with it," he replied.

"Good for you." I stood up. "I am thirsty, though. So I'm getting something if that's okay."

"Of course, it's okay. Everything is fine as long as you're comfortable. I'm here for you, not for me."

I grabbed a beer and hastened back to the couch.

"So, William told me you have experienced a panic attack after all that had happened," the doc started after I opened the can and took a first gulp of the malty cold liquid. "Actually, he said you had more than one."

The man didn't whip out a notebook and pen as I expected him to do. Instead, he just sat there, his hands on his knees, looking at me.

I took another sip before I answered. "Yeah... but I don't think it's that strange after all that has happened."

"Oh, not at all," he immediately replied. "I never called it strange. But I know these attacks are horrible to experience."

I couldn't disagree with that. "Yeah, I feel kinda shitty when it happens."

"When did the first one happen?"

"I've had a few when I was younger, but I got more and worse ones more recently because of Reggie. It started a few years back," I said, presuming that William and Gremelda had told the doc all about my crazy ex.

"What happened between the two of you?"

I rubbed my hands over my face a few times and then told Dr. Rosenfeld the same story as I'd told William and Spartacus.

It surprisingly felt good to talk to the man. He was very calm and understanding and not once did he make me feel as if I was a crazy person. I had been to a shrink after what happened between me and Reggie, and that psychiatrist was such an unpleasant experience. It was also the reason I didn't want to do this in the first place, but Dr. Rosenfeld seemed to be actually good at his job.

"So, you fear him?" he asked when I was done talking. "The reason the first attack started?"

"Well, yeah. It's pretty spooky if someone breaks into your home and just sits there on your couch or is taking a shower or lays in your bed. God only knows what he did in my house before I got home."

Even some of my panties had gone missing. Reggie apparently was such a sick prick that he stole my dirty underwear. It creeped me out so much. The thought I was ever willingly intimate with that man caused me to shiver all over. So disgusting. But I didn't tell Dr. Rosenfeld about it, for I was just incapable of pronouncing the words.

"What do you fear the most right now?" he asked. I had thought about this more often the last couple of days and I think it wasn't even my own life I feared for the most. I didn't want the people I cared about to end like Ramone and Mahindra. I didn't want more people to get killed because of me, and certainly not Dean or Shana.

"That Reggie is going to kill someone that I love."

Dr. Rosenfeld nodded. "Losing someone that you love is indeed one of the worst feelings in the world. And it's probably also the feeling that made Reggie respond so extremely," he said, grabbing the suitcase that stood beside him on the ground, a black rectangular leather case. "He lost you, the one he loved so much." He stopped talking and clicked open the two silver clasps, one by one. The sound pricked my ears while the rest of the room was completely silent. "And he simply couldn't handle that, which made him do the things he did."

The doctor looked into my eyes as he pulled something out of the suitcase. Something that made my blood run cold and robbed me of all air.

"...!"

WILLIAM

"Oh, for fuck's sake, how long have they been talking for already?" I asked Gremelda, pouring a third load of whiskey into my glass.

"About one und ein half hours," she answered. "It's not zat long yet."

It certainly felt fucking long. Tesla said she didn't feel the need to talk, but I guess she did.

I just wished this whole drama could be over as soon as possible. Apart from the fact that it wasn't good for my business, that fuck-face, Reggie, also made me look like a fool in front of my family, staff, and clients!

I love money and thus was sick about the fact this thing was costing me all the bets that were supposed to be placed at the Gladiator matches. We were talking about hundreds of thousands of dollars here. However, my pride was something I loved even more than money, and this man made me look as if I was some pathetic, weak, stupid twat. I was sure he was laughing at my face.

It was one man, for crying out loud. One! And he was outsmarting everyone!

I also felt bad for Tesla. I understood why my cousin had fancied the woman. She was very desirable with her big blue-green eyes and sexy soft round lips.

"Did you hear something about that lunatic's whereabouts already?" I asked the head of the security team. Eventually, Reggie was going to make a mistake. Right?

The moment Laurent went to respond, the phone rang. "It's Kevin," Laurent said.

Kevin was second in command.

"Put him on speaker," I ordered.

"Yeah, you're on speaker," Laurent said after he took the call.

"I have some bad news," Kevin started. "We've found another dead man in one of the boiler rooms. And this victim seems to have been dead for a long time already. If I were to take a guess, I would say at least three days. There was a bag over his head too. Fuck, man, I feel so bad for the guy."

"Oh, fucking hell!" I cried out, throwing my glass of whiskey against the wall, making the glass break into a thousand pieces. I couldn't believe he did it again. I felt anger, frustration, and a good amount of disappointment. "Who is the victim? Tell me now!" I impatiently asked.

"It's Dr. Rosenfeld, boss!"

CHAPTER 26

TESLA

"What-what is that thing?" I asked after Dr. Rosenfeld had taken a terrifying device out of his suitcase. I already knew the answer to my question, though. It was a fucking bomb. A small one, but a bomb nonetheless, made from explosives, wires and a timer that started ticking at 01:00:00 and straight away jumped to 00:59:59.

I wanted to cry for help, but the doctor held his finger in front of his mouth. "Shhhh." A warning for me to hold my tongue.

Why was he doing this? Was he working for Reggie?

He grabbed a remote control out of the suitcase next, and I was sure the noticeable red button on the clicker would set off the bomb when pressed. I sat paralyzed on the couch. Even if I wanted to scream, I couldn't do it. He smirked and stood up, walking towards me, and to my horror, he hung the bomb around my neck as if it was a fucking piece of jewelry.

"Hahhh...!" I gasped, looking down at the beeping device that pressed against my chest, ticking against my pounding ribcage.

I then looked up, into the pale blue eyes, and saw the man looking back at me with the creepiest expression on his face. How was it possible he'd transformed from that calm, sympathetic doctor into this scary, evil-looking criminal in just mere seconds?

Didn't these things only happen in shows? What the fuck was I going to do? Panicking, I looked around, knowing that there were a few guards in front of the door.

"Not a sound, Ryah, or I'll blow this entire building to pieces and you know I'll do it in a heartbeat."

Not the soft voice from before, but a different voice suddenly spilled from the man's lips.

A familiar voice.

My mouth popped open, and I started shaking my head as sweat started gushing from my pores.

"No."

No! This couldn't be!

"Oh, yes, my love. Have you missed me?" the man then asked, softly digging two fingers into his eye, plucking something out, which he dropped to the ground. My eyes followed the small transparent blue circle until it fell to the floor. A contact lens.

My heart skipped a beat.

"I have missed you, you know?" he said, pulling a lens from his other eye too.

Dr. Rosenfeld no longer had blue eyes but familiar dark brown ones.

Terror rushed through my veins, realizing the man I had been talking to for the past hour—the man I had just told all my feelings and thoughts and fears—was no other than the source of all these emotions!

"Reggie," I whispered.

"Bingo! Good afternoon, love," he enthusiastically said before he tore off a fake beard, making a fraction of his light brown skin to show itself. "At last, we meet again. How long has it been now?" he asked, pulling off a wig. "Oh, fuck, that's better. You do not know how much those things make your head itch."

"...!"

"I think it has been about a year or so?" he continued. "Give or take?"

"Take this thing off me, Reg!" I hissed.

"Nah," he replied, pulling the last chunks of latex off his face, transforming into the Reggie I remembered. "No fun if I do that," he added.

"Please don't do this," I all but begged. If this thing would go off, not only would I be blown to pieces, but Dean and Shana would be too. And all the other innocent people. I had to at least protect them!

"You have no idea how fucking easy this all was," he said, casually sitting on the chair again and smiling at me. "I actually killed the doc before that Indian guy. Both nice guys, by the way."

I felt tears filling my eyes.

"Oh, baby, are you feeling bad again? Because now there's yet another person dead because of you?" he asked.

"You did this," I pathetically responded. "I didn't want any of this."

"You were the one who left me, Ryah," he said, looking at me with dark, spine-chilling eyes before he started smiling again. "Anyway, as I was saying..." He grabbed my unfinished beer and took a gulp. "It was so freaking easy! Not only is the doc exactly my posture, but he also had this weirdass germ phobia, so I didn't even have to paint my hands! Look!"

He took off his gloves and avidly showed me his tattooed hands. "Please," I sobbed again.

"And," he continued, ignoring my pleas, "that William prick actually asked me why I sounded so weird, so I told him I had a cold—" Reggie couldn't continue for a minute because he was laughing so hard. "Haha, and he straightaway believed it! Girl, I'm just bummed out I wasn't able to see his face when they told him they found the psychiatrist's corpse in the boiler room. I've actually paid a client to tell them. If I'm correct, and my plan works, he already knows."

Reggie stood up and sauntered towards me, leaning in. His beer-smelling breath fanned against my face before he said, "Do you know why I wanted them to find the doc?" He looked at the timer. I did too. It said 00:55:46 now. "Because in about five to ten minutes, they'll burst into this room and they'll see you like this and know they've failed to keep you safe. Because in the end, I'm the only one that loves you enough to keep you safe. If I want to."

He brushed his lips against mine and then bit into my trembling bottom lip. It hurt and made me bleed. I could taste the iron.

"Damn, I've missed those sexy lips," he whispered into my mouth, licking them next. "I know you don't really mean all those lies you told about me. I know you missed my lips too."

"You're d-disgusting," I replied.

He started chuckling. "I also know you don't really mean that. D'you know I still watch our tape every day? You remember that night?"

I had never thought about that night again until now. We'd once taped ourselves having sex when things were still alright between us. Reggie wanted to scratch that off his bucket list, and I was so stupid to agree to it.

I felt myself getting nauseous. Beads of sweat rolled down my temples, and my legs were shaking while my heart pounded inside my throat.

"You moan so beautifully on that tape, baby."

I let out a little cry and wanted to take the bomb off my neck. "I'm getting this thing off, Reg. You're just bluffing," I hissed.

"I know you're fucking that Gladiator!" he hissed back, pulling my hands down again. "So you know I'm not bluffing at all. How could you stoop so low to let him fuck you? It's so gross, baby. Besides that, if I can't have you, he can't either. No one will. I'd kill you before I let anyone else have you. Now, that's real love."

"You're even sicker than I thought you were," I whisper-yelled.

He twisted my hands, and I was sure he just broke a few fingers as I heard a loud cracking sound and was in severe pain. I bit on my lips to stop myself from screaming out loud.

"Sick fucking psycho," I mumbled through the pain.

"Haha, oh, baby..." He pulled at my hair, making me look at him. "I pinned a note to the doc's body that if they want to save you, I want you standing outside, in front of the door, before this bomb goes off, so you can step into my car and we can leave together. I'll only disable this bomb if that happens. And if not?" He stood up straight and mimicked the sound of an explosion. "This whole place will explode into little bits, you and everyone with it."

"I'll go with you now," I quickly said, ignoring the drumming pain in my fingers. "We can go immediately." I wanted to leave this place as soon as possible. I didn't want Dean to get hurt.

"But, baby... where's the fun in that? Hm?" he asked. "I mean, I didn't spend more than twenty hours making this bomb for nothing, now did I? We have to make the best of it!"

I cried, still unable to fathom how all of this was happening. "Please, Reg!"

"Oh!" he said, tapping on his ear. I only now noticed he was wearing a listening device. "They're coming." He kissed me on the mouth. "It's showtime for me! And remember, if you or anybody else takes the bomb off, I'll end it all." He stuffed his listening device into my ear and headed towards the window. "Now, I can hear everything. See ya later, baby!"

"No, Reg! Reg!" I yelled in panic.

And away he was, disappearing out the window right before I heard multiple voices in the hallway, followed by a beep and then Dean and William burst through the door.

CHAPTER 27

SPARTACUS

Ryah, oh Ryah, oh fuck, Ryah. Please let her be okay. Please, please, please, please, please, I internally chanted while putting the keycard inside the slot with trembling sweaty fingers.

Never in my life had sweat gushed so fast out of my pores. Then again, I had never been this afraid before either.

"Hurry the fuck up!" William raised his voice and I wanted to slap him for it. I was fucking trying as best and fast as I could, fearing for life what I might find in my hotel room. Please let her be alright!

My heart slammed inside my chest, thinking about what Reggie could have done to her. Please, let her be alive.

After the beep, I threw my body against the door, busting it open, and for a split second, I was relieved, seeing her alive and still sitting at the same spot as where she'd sat when I left her. But then I saw her facial expression and something lighting up against her breasts. My eyes trailed lower, and I then realized what was hanging around her neck. It was a timer. Its bright red lights had caught my eyes.

It was a bomb!

Holy fucking Christ! Instant panic rose inside my chest as I rushed over to her, not caring about people seeing us together.

"OH, FUCK!" I cried out. "Baby, are you okay?!" She answered me with a sob.

"Jesus Christ!" William cursed.

Followed by Madame Gremelda who cursed something in German: "Oh mein Gott, dieses verdammte Arschloch!"

My first instinct was to pull the device from her body, but she shook her head, stopping my hands with hers, crying out that I wasn't allowed to touch it.

Laurent said the same before he asked Ryah, "Are you wired?"

Ryah nodded. "Yes, he can hear everything," she replied with a trembling voice.

"Fucking prick!" William hissed.

"There was a note pinned against the corpse," Kevin then said to me and all other people in the room. "We have to give her to that asshole before the timer ends."

"No fucking way!" I shook my head. No way we could do that.

"You need to get the fuck out of here! Right now! And take Shana with you!" Ryah shouted, her face wet with tears and beads of sweat, as her lips trembled in fear.

"I'm not going anywhere," I said and kneeled beside her. "I'm staying with you."

William then held his phone up. He had typed a message for us to read:

"Keep talking. Curse at us I have aa plan. stall hin."

He then fled the room together with Laurent and Gremelda while Kevin, a few other people from the safety team, and I waited with Ryah.

I tried to do what William ordered me. I cursed at Hotel Invicta for their failure to keep my baby safe. I reckoned it was a distraction for Reggie or something while they were arranging some other stuff.

I told Ryah it was gonna be alright, but all she did was keep telling me to leave. She wanted me to be safe. If we wouldn't have been in this shitty moment, I would have found it endearing. I could only hope that William knew what the fuck he was doing because, in the end, I knew we couldn't deny Reggie what he wanted or this bomb would set off. If that would happen, not only Ryah would die but many others with her: every soul in this hotel—innocent staff and clients too.

I grabbed Ryah's hand, making her hiss in pain.

"I-I think they're b-broken," she said, looking at her swollen bruised deformed fingers. I hadn't even noticed it. Shit, she must be in so much pain. Thinking about how Reggie had hurt her made my blood boil with anger. If I could, I would rip that sick fuck's head off.

I leaned in and gave Ryah kisses against her forehead, running my fingers through her hair. "You're so brave, you're doing so well, baby," I said.

The minutes that followed were the worst ones of my entire life. It felt as if it took ages for William to return. But then, finally, while the timer was at 00:40:35, he and the others quietly entered the room, together with an unfamiliar friendly face. She was a lady in her thirties, hair dyed in all the colors of the rainbow, matching her heavy make-up.

William held his finger in front of his mouth, a gesture for us to stay quiet about the sudden presence of the lady as she halted her steps in front of Ryah to inspect the bomb. Laurent, in the meantime, was doing something with a small black device together with the other members of William's team.

"Okay, you have one minute!" Laurent suddenly yelled. "We have blocked all incoming signals, so you now have eighty-five seconds before he'll be able to hear us again and will be able to set off the bomb. He can't do anything in the meantime!"

"Tesla, this is Candy, she's a client staying in the hotel and happens to be the number one bomb expert in our circles," William explained before he impatiently looked at Candy. "Can you disable this thing in under a minute?"

She nodded and opened her purse which was shaped like a cat, pink and glittery, and grabbed out a voltmeter and a small cable butter.

"Candy can't talk, so I vill talk for her. You have to sit as still as possible, Tesla," Madame Gremelda ordered, and I had never seen her look so anxious and scared before. I used to think she was incapable of showing fear. I felt my armpits gush as Candy started working.

Ryah herself was close to hyperventilating, so I went to stand behind her and laid my hands on her shoulders, leaned in, and breathed together with her as she tried to sit as still as possible.

"Only thirty seconds left!" Laurent shouted.

"Oh, fuck, fuck, fuck," Ryah whispered. "You have to leave, please leave, all of you, please, please."

"We're not going anywhere, okay?"

She let out a sob.

"Twenty seconds left!"

Jesus, this countdown fucking didn't help. I saw Ryah balling her fists.

"Candy, baby!" William yelled as he paced through the room, his hands running through his hair. "You gotta hurry the hell up!"

"Fifteen!"

Candy looked up and nodded at William.

"You're done?" he asked, to which she nodded again. "You're sure about this?" he asked, and the room was completely silent except for Ryah's ragged breaths.

Candy signed something with her hands.

"Ten!" Laurent's heavy voice bounced off the wall.

"She is certain for about eighty percent," Madame Gremelda answered.

"What the hell, Candy, what happens during the other twenty percent?"

"FIVE!"

Candy made a sign with her index finger, a gesture of slitting her throat. Even though our throats wouldn't get slit, I think it was pretty clear what she meant would happen to us. We would all fucking die. There was a chance we would all fucking die and William had to call the shots. I didn't envy him.

"THREE!"

"Okay. Fuck it! Do it, Candy!"

She cut one of the wires, making the bomb stop at while the red lights turned to a shade of neon green.

"Fucking hell!" William shouted while multiple sighs from the others filled my ears. My thoughts exactly.

Ryah started to cry, all emotions coming out.

"Thank you," she said to Candy more than once.

Candy patted her shoulder, eyes looking at Ryah with sympathy before she took the bomb away from her neck and stuffed it in her glitter kitty purse.

"Definitely, thank you," I also told her. This woman just saved all our lives and I wished I could say more than that since words didn't feel enough.

William yanked the listening device out of Ryah's ear and left with the rest, leaving me and Ryah behind with only Madame Gremelda.

"What the fuck is he going to do?" I asked, cocking my head to the boss.

"During zee time Reggie wasn't able to track us, we were able to track him," she explained. "So, William is going to get him. You both stay here. We'll talk about zis relazionship later." She pointed from me to Ryah and back at me again. "But for now, I'll leave you with her to comfort her while I'll get some medical help."

"Thank you," Ryah said.

Gremelda gave her a small nod and left.

"Jesus, baby." I dropped to my knees in front of her and looked at her fingers. "Everything is alright again."

"I was so s-scared," she replied with a trembling voice. "I just wanted you to leave. I couldn't bear the thought of you dying because of this."

"I didn't die, you didn't die. And you heard Gremelda, this time they have him. He made a mistake, being too bold to do this, and now he'll repay for hurting you."

She pushed her lips against mine and kissed me hard before she pressed her forehead against mine. "You're the only therapist I'll ever need from now on."

I couldn't help but laugh as she did too, all tension coming out. It was scary to look death into the eyes and we both came pretty fucking close today, but we would be alright. I could feel it.

Chapter 28

TESLA

Yesterday, the doctor confirmed that my fingers were indeed broken. To get the best care, he'd ordered me to get an X-ray. Hotel Invicta wouldn't be Hotel Invicta if there wasn't a small hospital wing in here. So that's where Dean and I went, accompanied by Madame Gremelda.

The doctor had taped together two broken fingers with a splint after he set them straight. Luckily, he told me that no surgery was required. My fingers would heal over time.

After everything that happened, I tried to leave this whole Reggie thing in William's hands, as Gremelda ordered me to, but I found myself looking over my shoulder the whole time I was out of my room. Luckily Dean was there with me, plus a few guards, but still... That feeling of Reggie suddenly appearing stayed with me.

Presently, I was laying in my own bed, cuddling up against a familiar warm body. Apart from yesterday, Dean was also allowed to stay with me for the next few days, something I was beyond grateful for. I wondered why we were allowed to, but my guess was that Madame Gremelda pitied me.

Dean was the only one I truly wanted to be with right now. I needed him, maybe even more than I needed Shana. I felt safe around him. I guess that was something this whole thing had taught me: I liked him. I already did before, but I was really falling for the Gladiator by now.

"Are you comfortable like this?" he asked the same way he'd asked an hour ago and the hour before that.

He held me and spooned me from behind, his whole body against mine. I was so tired and with the painkillers I had been on since yesterday, I slept most of the day, which was more than welcome right now.

"Hmm-hmm," I hummed back.

How could I not fall for him?

When I woke up from my afternoon nap, my face was half-buried somewhere in his left armpit. It took some time before I realized where I was and that what had happened was real and not a nightmare I just woke up from.

Dean noticed my anxiety going to a high level, so he quickly held me tight in his muscular arms. "It's okay. You're here with me, it's just us."

This had happened two times already, me waking up in a panic. I really fucking wanted it to be over now.

"Okay, sorry." I took a big breath. "Ugh, fucking hell."

After I'd caught my breath back, I lost it again when he said: "They caught him. I got the message half an hour ago."

"They-they did?" I asked.

"Yeah, he... is dead."

I felt weird, not sure what to think of it. What if he wasn't dead but had deceived everyone again? But on the other hand... what if he really was dead? Was I happy about that? Was I relieved?

"Oh," was all I said. "Is William sure?"

"The message sounded like he was one hundred percent sure," Dean replied. I took a big breath and exhaled through my nose before I laid my head down on top of one of his muscled pecs. "William also said you can see for yourself, see if it's really him," he softly said. "If you want, I can come with you?"

"Jesus, I don't know if I want that."

"I understand."

"I'm sorry, it's all so fucking insane," I said.

"It is," he agreed. "It's like we're caught in a movie."

"Yeah, like some fucking bad action movie featuring Stephen Seagull or something."

He chuckled. "Stephen seagull?"

"Yeah."

"It's Seagal, darling. Not seagull, haha."

"Whatever." I smiled too. "My dad always watched that crap."

"Hey! I happen to like that man's crap! I've seen every movie he starred in. Especially when I was younger."

"Oh, my God. Horrible."

It felt good not to think about serious shit for a moment. I knew Dean could sense I needed this. He kissed the top of my head and grabbed me in his arms.

"Officially, I need another four months to save enough money for my brother's surgery, but when I'm done, I want to get out of here and... well... uh, I want us to see each other in a normal environment too. How about you?"

"I'd like that too."

"You do?"

I nodded against his chest. "Yup."

"That makes me so fucking happy, Ryah." I felt his heart beating faster and faster against my cheek. The little chest hair he had pricked against my skin.

He was such a good guy.

"Do you think we're allowed to stay?" I asked. "I mean they now know we didn't follow the rules."

"I don't know."

"What's that," I asked after William put a large black box in the middle of the coffee table.

"Reggie's head," he answered matter-of-factly.

"Jesus, what the fuck?! Uh, I mean... I'm sorry, I didn't mean to curse."

"Boss, I don't think—"

"Shut up, Spartacus," William ordered. "Tesla, I think you should look, or this guy's presence will hunt you for the rest of your life. You can act all cool, but trust me, you won't find peace until you know absolutely sure he is dead. And you will only be absolutely sure if you can see it for yourself."

"And if I look at a human's head, don't you think I'll get hunted by that image my whole life?"

"It's better that than to live in fear." He looked at me with sharp eyes, an expression that made it clear he wouldn't take no for an answer. I was going to look into that box whether or not I wanted to.

"I think he is right, though," Dean said. I looked at him. "You should look and be done with this shit so you can close this horrible time. And... looking in that box might give you that closure, even if it's hard to do."

"I never wanted anybody to die. Not even Reggie. I never—"

"I know," Dean said. "But what happened, happened. Time can not be turned back, but if you've found closure, you at least wouldn't have to turn your head every time you're not locked up in a room with a couple of men guarding the place."

William grabbed the lid of the box and took it off. "I'm sure it's him. I just want you to be sure as well."

I couldn't believe I was actually going to listen to them, but I found myself standing up to peek into the box.

"...!"

Oh, that was Reggie alright.

Nausea rose inside of me when I looked at his severed head. His eyes were closed, but his mouth was slightly open and he looked so... so... dead. I would have thrown up if William hadn't closed the box.

"It's h-him," I said with a trembling voice and sat down again before I fainted. "What-what happened?" I asked.

"We tracked him down in that one minute he wasn't able to hear us or could control the bomb. I only dared to execute that plan because I knew Candy was staying with us. I certainly wouldn't have trusted anybody else with that bomb. Because he said you were to stand outside for him, we knew he couldn't be far. Turned out he was hiding in the building next to Invicta. We found him soon, but the asshole escaped again. We finally caught him this morning."

"And you... killed him then?"

"Obviously."

Yeah, I had to agree it was a dumb question.

"Uh... how?" I did not know why I asked. The word just spilled from my lips and I instantly regretted it. "Never mind, I don't want to know."

"I wouldn't have shared it, anyway. Someone so innocent that she's almost puking just by looking at a dead man's head isn't ready to hear any details."

"What about us?" I asked him as I looked at Dean and back at William again.

"Ah, yes, you two..." William stood up. "We'll discuss that later when you've processed all of this, but... I think you know how I feel when it comes to rules that are broken."

Chapter 29

TESLA

"How are you doing?" William asked, stirring chopsticks into the cardboard box his assistant had brought over.

It was just me and him, sitting in his office at three o'clock in the afternoon, one week after the whole Reggie drama. It was the first time we have had a private conversation because the boss had been gone for the past week, probably doing some underworld stuff.

"I'm doing pretty okay," I answered, nervously bouncing my leg up and down. I was just waiting for him to start talking about Dean and me.

"Your fingers?" he then asked, nudging his head to my still wrapped up fingers.

"They're healing properly. No more pain either."

"That's good." He brought chopsticks to his mouth and took another bite. The scent of it made my stomach grumble. "Very good. And the panic attacks?"

"Better. I've only had one, and that was like three days ago, after a nightmare. I'm really doing fine. I think I'm ready to get back to work again."

I was sick and tired of sitting in the hotel room, doing nothing. Gremelda and the doctor had said I should rest first and heal, but I would rather see the Gladiator matches and hang out with the rest. I even missed Mercedes's grumpy bitch face. Reggie was dead and they delivered his dead body (and head) to the police, so why couldn't I just move on with how life was before? Luckily, Shana was allowed to visit me. At least that gave some fun.

"Back to work?" William asked, raising a brow.

"Well... uh... yeah?"

"You call fucking your secret boyfriend working? You call getting a thousand bucks as a bonus to do that, on top of your free stay here in the hotel work?" He took another bite, slurping the noodles between his lips.

Okay, now that he said it like that....

I cleared my throat. "Well..." Awkwardly scratching the back of my neck, I couldn't come up with a suitable answer to that question.

Was he going to fire me now? Fire Dean? Or the both of us? Was he going to give us a scolding for breaking his rules? Something worse?

"Tell me, have you even once read your contract?" William asked very calmly.

"Uh... I have to admit I haven't completely read the whole thing," I replied. "I mean, it was as thick as the bible."

"My lawyers do love to make some thick contracts. If you would have read it more carefully, you would have noticed there also is a section in there about breaking the rules."

"A... section?" I asked, suddenly feeling nervous. Damn it! Why had I been so stupid to not read it completely?

"Hmm-hmm," he hummed before he took another slurp and then wiped his chin, purposely making me wait for his answer. "Page fifteen, section three."

"Oh..." I swallowed.

"Yup." He scraped the inside of his meal box for the last bite. "You want to know what it says?" he asked when he was done eating.

I nodded.

"It says that I'm allowed to break one bone for each broken rule. Tesla... I mean, crap. I find this very unfortunate now that your fractures are just healing up nicely."

"Y-you're shitting me," I said, stuttering. "That's not what the contract says."

I couldn't imagine he would do this to me. I knew guests were punished severely for breaking rules, but I was part of Invicta's staff. Come on! But then again, I also couldn't imagine he would joke around about torturing me at a time like this, would he? Especially not about broken bones.

"I'm actually not shitting you." He opened his drawer and pulled out a contract. My contract. "Page fifteen," he said again.

I quickly grabbed the stack of papers and turned the pages until I found the page he'd said. It was fucking true. It stood there, written in black. I looked at William, who looked back at me, wearing a stupid grin on his face. "See?" he asked.

"...!"

"Now, I bet you two haven't been screwing around once or twice. You've done it a lot. So... I guess I have a lot of bones to break, Tesla. A lot of bones."

"You're fucking with me! Aren't you?"

"Am I?"

"I-It's not Dean's f-fault!"

"It's not?"

I shook my head, my lungs already asking for special attention. No way I was going to hyperventilate in front of that man again. He was just playing with me! I trusted William since day one, although I didn't know why I did since he was a mobster. Still, I trusted him.

He started chuckling. "Okay, okay. I will not break your bones."

"And Spartacus, you're not going to—"

"I'll spare that lucky bastard too." He sighed. "Not that you both deserve that."

"So, you were fucking with me? Why would you do that?!" I raised my voice, visibly irritated.

"Cause I'm an asshole, Tesla. You know that."

"You're an asshole right now, yes. But you're not an asshole usually. You helped me with everything. I'll be forever grateful for that."

"Just so you know, I can fuck you for real too." He smirked.

"I don't want that."

"Booooring. Oh, well, I thought I could at least try my luck, since you're into breaking the rules, anyway."

I smiled at him. "Thank you," I said.

He grabbed the contract again and put it in the drawer. "There will be a change from now on, though. I let this go because we suffered some strange times. But after all this bullshit, I have to get back my client's trust—"

"I'm sorry—"

"Shut up," he cut me off.

"Ok."

"Which means Hotel Invicta has to be the best again. I won't allow any rules to be broken again. Not by you, not by Spartacus, not by your pretty little friend. By nobody, or I'll have to crack some ribs, and I truly don't want to do that to my own staff because ultimately, it'll only cost me money." I didn't know if I was allowed to speak so I nodded at him before he continued. "I'm not fucking Santa Claus handing out money and bonuses only for you to bang my number one Gladiator. If you want to work here, you'll bang, lick feet, and suck dick from whoever chooses you as a Rewarder, whether you like him or not. And to test the both of you, I'll make sure Spartacus won't fight every match so that on the days he isn't fighting, you'll serve whoever chooses you. If you can't fucking handle that, you're free to leave my company."

"Sounds fair..." I whispered as I couldn't argue with him. He made perfect sense.

"Fuck! You think he also knows about what happened between me and Gannicus?!" Shana asked before she nervously bit into her bottom lip until it was red.

We both sat on my couch like good old times, my feet laying on her lap, both of us wearing sweats.

"I think he does. But I also think he'll let it slide this time," I answered.

"Fuck. Okay, I hope so. Because this body is too good to be flawed, girl. And I was just getting my mojo back!" Shana said. "You should have seen Gannicus. First, he was all like, 'no, we aren't gonna do anything', and by the end of the week, he was like putty in my hands."

I laughed. "I'm sure he was."

"But... what will you do now?" she asked, looking serious.

"I think... I want to make things between me and Dean work. I learned that in the past few weeks. So, I don't want to sleep with others. I also think Dean will lose it if I do and I don't want him to get hurt. He's kind of a great guy."

"I'm happy for you."

"Me too."

"And he has no more crooked teeth or orangutan arms either—"

"Shana!" I yelled, making her chuckle. I hit her shoulder with my good hand. "Shut the fuck up, or I swear—"

"It's just fun to tease you. I've missed that." I knew she had it hard too, especially when she heard what had happened to me. "Anyway," she continued, "what does this all mean?"

"I guess it means I'm going to have to quit my job?"

Chapter 30

TESLA

"But-but you just got here." Shana looked at me with a pout.

"Yeah, it was a very brief career."

"I understand you want to give your relationship a chance, though."

"You could join me. We could get out together."

She seemed to think about it for a bit.

"I've always planned to keep doing this until I've saved a certain amount and I'm not there yet. Plus, I like this job, so I want to stay... But things seriously won't be the same without you." She sighed, patting my knees. "I've been spoiled by your presence. Ugh! Hey! Can't you ask William for another job here? Like, you could join the cleaning staff! They stay at another wing of the hotel, but we could at least call that way."

"I'm tempted but no... I really think I want to leave, Shana. In this hotel, it's not only you and Dean, who are the most amazing people to have in my life, but here, this place... this is also the place of Mahindra's death and the whole Reggie thing. I really like the idea of starting fresh, you know?"

"I'm just worried that—"

"You don't have to be worried. How long are you planning on staying?"

"Another year," she answered.

"Fuck, that's still so long, woman!" This time it was me doing the whining.

It had been a crazy day. First I talked with William, then chatted with Shana, then I visited Gremelda's office and now I was about to have a serious talk with Dean.

We sat at the bar, and he looked so confused.

When I'd told him we had to meet in the bar, he already didn't get why we couldn't just meet in one of our rooms and I just told him the reason: that I talked with William and that we couldn't go on with what we were doing.

"Okay, so now what?" Dean asked. He looked at me with the saddest, largest puppy eyes ever as he continued, "I mean, I understand William. I understand that there are rules, but... Ugh, it fucking sucks! Let's just quit together." Frustrated, he took a sip from his tall glass of milk, and, for some reason, I got all warm inside. Only he could look this cool drinking a glass of fucking milk in a bar!

"No. You have to stay," I answered. "You said you needed another four months to gain the money for your brother's surgery and I don't want to stand in the way. But I need to leave. I handed Madame Gremelda my resignation letter just an hour ago."

"You what?" He looked at me in surprise. "Before we even discussed anything?"

"Yup," I replied. "If it would be useful, I would have waited, but there was nothing to discuss, Spartacus. I leave or I'll serve others, it's that simple."

"I guess. Fuck. I also don't like to hear you call me that way again," he said.

We sat there for a bit, just looking at each other until he broke the silence.

"So, what did she say?"

"She wasn't thrilled, but she understood my decision. Honestly, it's just time for me to live my normal life again. I came to Invicta because of all the shit that was going on and because I needed money. And those two things have been taken care of. William handled Reggie and the people coming after me, and I've made a small amount of savings that will help me out for about two months, leaving me enough time to look for another job."

"I don't want you to leave and be all by yourself."

"I'm not alone. I have my family outside, you know? I can turn to them if things are hard. Nobody is chasing me anymore and I hardly have any nightmares."

"You said that was because you slept beside me."

"I did. But I'm a big girl, Dean. Reggie is dead and I swear I can take care of myself. Besides that, what is your ideal solution, then? You want to help your brother, right?"

"Of course, I do—"

"Well, then. I have decided. I'll leave, you'll stay. We will stay faithful to each other and meet up when you're out."

"We can't even call," Dean said, discreetly folding his hand around mine under the bar.

"We can set a date where to meet when you're out," I replied.

"We can't even fuck one last time." He bit his lip.

"Yeah... that's a bummer," I agreed, already getting hot just by looking at his mouth. "But the boss was quite clear and I don't want to step over his boundaries again. Especially not after all he has done for me."

Dean sighed, squeezing my hand. "I know... When will you leave?"

"Tonight."

"Tonight?!"

"In three hours, actually."

"In three hours?!" He gasped.

I smiled at him. I fucking hated leaving him too. But it was only for a while. And it was for a good cause.

"Who will you choose when I'm gone?" I asked. I needed to keep talking or I might get emotional.

"Cedi," he answered. I slapped his shoulder as hard as I could, but I think it was only my hand that ended up in pain. Luckily, it wasn't my broken hand. "Of course, I won't, darling," he quickly said, chuckling. "I guess I'll pick nobody. There isn't a rule that forces me to pick, and I don't want anybody but you."

"That's the better answer." God, I wanted to kiss him so badly.

"Can I help you pack?"

"I'm afraid not. Can't come into my room, remember? I can only hang out with other Rewarders."

"Unfair." He was so bummed out. "Fuck, Ryah. So, when we leave the bar, that's it?"

"Come on... it's only for four months. Don't be so dramatic, dude," I replied, even though I felt my throat closing at the thought of missing him. I quickly took my last gulp of beer.

"Let's have another drink then. Are we at least allowed to do that?" he asked, annoyed.

"We are."

If I was quick, I could be finished with packing in an hour anyway.

I was home again. Home, in my own apartment. It felt so weird, and not at all like home.

The place had been cleaned up and someone had replaced all the broken items. This had to be William's doing. Just by looking at the new furniture, I could already tell this was way more expensive stuff than what I'd previously owned. And I had to admit, I liked the style.

After I'd taken a shower and dropped on my new dark red leather couch, my phone went off. I took the call. "Hello?"

"You like the new interior?"

"Hi, William. You are too generous, really. But, yeah, I love it."

"Not really. Your man is going to refuse any Rewarder from now on, so that saved me a lot of thousand-dollar bonuses. See, this as a gift from him. You don't think I would pay money that's not needed, do you? Who do you take me for?"

I smiled. What a weird mobster this man was. "Thank you, anyway."

"Sure. Have you returned safely?"

"I have." I laid down on my couch. It even smelled of real leather.

"Good."

"But are you allowed to call me? Invicta people can't talk with the outside world," I reminded him.

"I'm out of the hotel. Business trip."

"Ah."

"Anyway..." It was silent for a while. "That was all I wanted to know. I'll tell Gremelda too. She might look like a bitch, but she was worried."

"I know she's not a bitch."

I heard his breathing until he said, "Gotta go."

"Ok. Thanks again."

He cut the call, making me wonder if this was the last time I'd ever speak to him. It felt weird somehow if it was.

The rest of the evening, I tried to watch some shows on tv, but I had no interest in them. I already missed Dean. Was this what it felt like to be in love? I wondered if I had ever felt it before. Of course, I had liked some guys, but I was actually willing to sacrifice my life for Dean. I wondered if I would have done the same for my exes. I know for a fact Dean would sacrifice his life for me too and I also wondered if my exes would have done that.

I knew I talked big this afternoon, but I was kind of scared to sleep alone again. I had been so pampered by sleeping in his arms that I didn't want to sleep alone anymore. I got cold just thinking about it.

"Oh, come on," I told myself. "Stop with this wallowing."

Dean would get out soon and I had four months to plan the most amazing reunion ever. I know I'd told him to ask me out on a date, but maybe it was me who should do it. It would only be fair.

31

Epilogue

SPARTACUS

The past four months had passed by at a snail's pace, but today was finally the day. My last day as a Gladiator and my last day spending in Hotel Invicta!

Was I going to miss Crixus, Gannicus, Cedi, Gremelda, and all others? Sure, I would. They had been my family during my stay here and some of us had grown pretty close. But even so, I longed to get out more than anything. I wanted to return to my real family. I'd missed my parents and brother for years, and even though Ryah had only been gone for a few months, I missed her just as much. Not being able to call or see her was fucking horrible. I missed her touch, her kisses, her voice, her smile. Everything.

I don't know how many times my cock and hand had been best buddies lately, but they saw each other a lot.

"Man, I can't believe you're really going to leave us tomorrow and that tonight will be our last fight together!" Crixus yelled before he punched me in the nose during this last training session.

"What are you trying to do? Making me look ugly on purpose before I get out? Cut it out, man," I said, wiping the blood away.

"It's not his fault you're already at home in your mind. Pay some fucking attention during your last day, will you?" Oenomaus yelled from the other side of the arena.

"I'm sorry," I answered since I had to admit he was right. I was busy with all kinds of things instead of training.

"You want to leave with a bang, don't you? Or would you rather lose your last match?" Oenomaus asked.

"I won't lose!" I replied before I knocked my fist against Crixus's jaw, who went straight down after the blow.

"That's the spirit!" Oenomaus answered. I would miss him, too.

That evening, the team organized a small goodbye party for me, just as Ryah had received when she'd left. It was nothing fancy, just a small get-together in the bar as we were all tired after the match.

Oenomaus had made me fight a special scene tonight as a farewell gift. Not one, but two other men had to fight me while I was blindfolded. It wasn't an honest match at all, even though they were our lowest-ranked players. I won, though Oenomaus was still an asshole to do that to me on my last day. I take back my words; I would not miss him at all.

"Bye, buddy. It was an honor to train you," he said, patting my shoulder. Okay, I take back my words again. I would miss him.

"The pleasure was all mine. I've learned so much from you," I replied, repaying him with a hug. "Thank you."

After Oenamous, I said goodbye to the others.

"Crixus, Gannicus," I said, looking at the two. "You were my family in here, and I'm going to miss you guys the most. Thank you for this crazy adventure." I hugged them and we promised each other we would meet again somewhere in this lifetime. It was kind of cute to see Crixus with teary eyes, even though he said he was tearing up because a fly flew in his eyes. Really, man?

"Cedi," I said, standing before her. "Can I get a hug?"

We had cleared things between us about three months ago and things were back to normal again. Without the fucking, of course! I hadn't laid a finger on another person. But Cedi at least didn't look at me like she wanted to kill me anymore.

"Of course," she replied, and then hugged me.

"Be sweet to Crixus."

They weren't allowed to be together, but at least they had their private moments.

"Always," she said, breaking the hug.

Bentley stood beside us, holding something in her hands. She waited till Cedi had left and stood far enough so she wouldn't be able to hear us.

"I'm sure we'll meet again, Dean," she whispered, winking. "Can you give this to her?" she asked. "Please?" It was a folded sheet of paper she held, no doubt a letter. I took it out of her hands. "And please tell her I miss her?"

"I'll tell her."

"Good." Bentley sniffed. "That's good."

That evening, we drank and we laughed and we thought of all the things we had been through together. It was around one o'clock we called it quits and left for our rooms. I was so ready to sleep in this bed alone for the last time.

I couldn't wait till it was morning!

"Spartacus," Madame Gremelda said as we stood in front of the door that led outside—a door I hadn't used in a long while. "I hope zat life be good to you."

"Gremelda, I will miss your German accent."

She laughed. "Goodbye."

And that was it. No hug, no handshake. She hadn't attended the small goodbye party yesterday either, but the fact she walked with me to the entrance during my last minutes here was enough for me. She cared that I left. And she was going to miss me.

Gremelda, the ice queen.

I watched her until she was out of sight before I turned to the guard, and while wearing a huge grin on my face, I asked him to open the door. It was sunny outside, the sunrays warming my face as I stepped outside.

There she was, standing on the sidewalk before Invicta's entrance, looking at me with familiar green-blue eyes, mouth curling up in a smile. I rushed over to her and held her tight.

Fucking finally.

"Darling, I missed you so much," I said before kissing the top of her head.

"I missed you too, but you're-you're s-squeezing too t-tight," she stuttered. "C-can't breathe."

I laughed and kissed her on her lips. Ryah kissed me back with the same amount of passion, both of us not giving a rat's ass that people might see us.

"How have you been, babe?" I asked after I'd pulled my tongue from her mouth. "I need to know everything."

I wanted to hear everything, but I also wanted to feel everything. Jesus, I could just eat her up or crawl under her skin!

"Let's go to my place," she whispered hoarsely into my ear. "I'll tell you everything you want to hear. After..."

"After?" I asked.

"After you've fucked me."

"For now, I'm working in this lunchroom slash restaurant called Papa Jojo's," Ryah said as she rested on my chest. "It doesn't pay much, but it gives me space to maybe go back to school, cause Jojo and I agreed I'll only do day shifts, so I work from eleven to seven. It's not really a job to be proud of, cause they've only chosen me because of my looks. But whatever, it's at least something and my colleagues are nice."

"You want to go back to school?" I asked curiously, running my fingers over her spine.

She felt even better than I remembered.

"It's just something going through my head," she replied.

"You should go for it."

"Yeah?

"Hmm-hmm."

"What will you do now you're out of William's claws?" she asked.

"First, I want to visit my parents and brother tomorrow," I answered. "Care to join me?"

"...!"

"Too soon?" I asked after I saw her confused eyes looking up at me.

"Maybe a little bit," she answered, resting her head on my chest again.

"You're right. I haven't seen them for so long, so all my attention must go to them. I just... am not liking the thought of lying to them about where I'd been and I know I'm going to have to do that."

Hotel Invicta even gave all staff members an entire collection of expertly photoshopped photos of people around the Eiffel Tower,

Niagara Falls, Taj Mahal, and whatever else we needed to tell them about our so-called trip around the world.

"It was alright for me," Ryah answered. "I mean... I'm not proud of lying to all the people, but you and I, and all the others in Invicta, all knew that this was going to happen when we signed up. Don't feel too guilty; just think about all the money you collected! Thanks to you, your brother will get his surgery!"

"I guess." I truly was thankful for that. "I think I'm going to say that I hit the jackpot in Vegas."

"And after you visited them, how will normal life look like then?"

"I dunno..." I answered. "But William called me at the last-minute and said that I could return for fights. Not on a full-time basis, but every four or six months, or so. He said I could stay for two weeks or a month."

"Oh, he said that?"

"He did. And even though I'll probably die from missing you, I'm thinking about it, because I can earn a year's worth of average salary there in one month."

"That's true."

"Yeah, though it was kinda lame he told me after I said farewell to everyone."

Ryah chuckled. "Let's not think about Invicta right now."

"Agreed. Now, all I want to think about is you. Oh, by the way, Bentley sent you something."

After Ryah read the letter, we had another round of fucking because she was a little sad about missing her friend so it was my cock's duty to make her feel better again.

"You taste salty," she said, whispering against my lips.

"Well... someone let me work pretty hard today, making me sweat buckets...."

She chuckled as she let her finger run over my skin. "We should get out of bed now, though. I have planned a surprise for you...."

"Wait till I say you can look."

After Ryah took the blindfold off, a cool breeze hit my still closed eyelids.

During the car ride, she'd forbidden me to take the black ribbon from my eyes for the last sixty minutes. I wanted to do it, though, because this thing took me back to those dreadful blindfolded fights. However, she didn't give in, not even after my whining.

I wondered what she had planned because she had been cursing for the last ten minutes. About how 'things weren't supposed to be like this'.

Standing there with my eyes still closed, I heard kids playing in the background, cars passing by in the further distance, and lots of people chatting and walking around us. There was the fragrance of roasted meat and something sweet. Maybe cotton candy?

"Are we at a carnival or something?" I asked.

"Not really... Okay, you can look now," she answered.

"Finally." I opened my eyes, and the first thing I saw was the cause of the scent: a tiny food truck that sold hamburgers a few meters further behind a fence. We stood in the middle of a bunch of market stalls while lots of people passed us by.

"So... this wasn't how I'd planned it. I didn't know something was going on here today," she said. "It's some kind of festival."

"...?"

And then I saw the hooped ring hanging above me. We were standing at the sports courts. The basketball court to be precise. This was the basketball court.

"Anyway... I planned something, and it's kinda ruined now."

I smiled. "The last time we stood on this particular basketball court was almost nine years ago."

"Well, duh. That was my whole point. I just didn't plan on sharing the place with hundreds of other people—"

"Whoa!" I had to dodge a ball that some toddler with a green booger hanging out of his nose nearly kicked against my nose. I caught it in time and threw it back to him, earning myself a smile.

When the kid was gone, Ryah grabbed my hands. "Anyway. It's time to redeem myself. Dean Matthew Caddel, would you like to date me?" She bit her lip. "If you want to take revenge, you can say no."

I chuckled. "Why the fuck would I say no?"

"I have no fucking idea, but I'm still not one hundred percent sure you're gonna forgive me and say yes."

"Well, Ryah Boone, I say yes." I grabbed her and kissed her. Just a peck this time. I mean, kids were watching and all that.

She cuddled me. "Phew. And," she said, pushing me away to grab something from her pocket, "this is for you too."

It was a little metal card. A USB-stick. "Thanks, babe."

"It has all my favorite songs, but it doesn't spell 'Thanks for going out with me'."

"It doesn't? Well, that's a disappointment," I answered, feigning being very displeased.

She wrapped her arms around my neck and again craned her head, whispering into my ear:

"No, it doesn't. But it does spell something that you desperately want me to do. Something we haven't tried yet..."

My heart rate sped up. "Oh, now I'm curious, darling."

She laughed. "So, what do you want to do? Stay here? Check this festival out, or—"

"Nope. I want to go home," I said, grabbing her hand in mine. "I need to listen to those songs right now!" I added as she entangled our fingers together.

Eight years ago, I left this basketball court in sadness because of a girl named Ryah. But this time, there was no sadness in my heart. There was only love as we left this place together, knowing that life was yet to begin. And that was a beautiful prospect.